# Outback Dawn: The Visitor

## ANNIE SEATON

The Augathella Girls: Book 5

# ANNIE SEATON

*ISBN 978-0-6454843-3-5*

# Dedication

*To those who travel the back roads and discover little gems of towns like Augathella.*

ANNIE SEATON

# The Augathella Girls series.

**Book 1: Outback Roads –The Nanny**

**Book 2: Outback Sky – The Pilot**

**Book 3: Outback Escape – The Sister**

**Book 4: Outback Winds – The Jillaroo**

**Book 5: Outback Dawn – The Visitor**

**Book 6: Outback Moonlight – The Rogue**

**Book 7: Outback Dust – The Drifter**

**Book 8: Outback Hope – The Farmer**

# Augathella Characters-Book 5

| | |
|---|---|
| Laura Adnum | Braden's sister-in-law |
| Harry Higgins | Town doctor |
| Bec Hunter | Nurse |
| Sophie Cartwright | Station Cook |
| Kent Mason | Sophie's fiancé |
| Braden Cartwright | Sophie's brother |
| Callie Young | Braden's partner |
| Jon Ingram | Station Manager |
| Fallon Malone | Helicopter pilot |
| Ruth Malone | Fallon's mother |
| Jacinta Mason | Kent's sister |
| Amelia Foley | Station hand |
| Ben Riley | Shire Engineer |

# Chapter 1

*The Pub*

Braden put his arm around Callie's shoulder and looked around, satisfied at what he saw. His sister, Sophie, caught his eye and her smile was wide as she looked back at him. Her fiancé, Kent, was deep in conversation with Jon Ingram, and Fallon was sitting at the end of the table, one hand on her very pregnant stomach. Kent's sister, Jacinta, sat beside Sophie's best friend, Kimberly, and a couple of their teacher friends from the primary school were at the other end of the table with their partners, all local cattlemen Braden had worked with.

The queue at the bistro was growing quickly and Callie leaned into him. 'Do you think we should wait for Ben and Amelia, or should we order?'

Braden gestured to the door. 'Here they are now. I'd say Ben took Amelia for a drive to show her what he's bought.'

'Has he got a new car?'

'Nope. He's bought a house. George Malone's place. Ruth and her husband have finished here and they're going back to Brisbane for a month or so until the baby's born.'

Callie elbowed him in the ribs. 'How come I work in town but you know more gossip than I do?'

'Because I'm a local.' He pressed his lips close to her ear. 'And you could be too if you agreed to set a wedding date.'

He felt Callie's withdrawal and a chill ran through him. He just hoped it wasn't a premonition.

'Don't push, Bray. I agreed to stay engaged, but we won't get married until we're sure it's the right thing for the boys.'

'I'm sorry, sweetheart. I love you, and I want you to be my wife.'

'And I've said yes, but when Nigel's better.'

Kent stood up and dinged a spoon on the side of his beer glass. It was barely heard over the noise in the bistro, so he put two fingers to his mouth and whistled.

Instant silence fell over their table and across the whole bistro.

'Ssh, everyone, Kent's gonna sing us a song,' came a quavering voice from the bar.

'I'll sing you a song, Reggie,' he replied with a laugh. 'Thanks for coming, everyone. Sophie and I just wanted to say a few words while we had you all together, and before we all start eating.'

Sophie stood up and took Kent's hand and satisfaction filled Braden. His sister was settled, and she had a good man back in her life.

'Thanks, everyone,' Sophie echoed Kent's words. 'Ta-da! Kent and I have set a wedding date.'

Cheers and clapping filled the room, and she waited for the noise to subside before she continued. 'September three, the first Saturday in spring. And three lovely ladies have agreed to be my bridesmaids. Stand up, girls!'

Kimberly Riordan was the first to stand and another cheer went up. Kent's sister, Jacinta stood slowly, her cheeks flushed with embarrassment. Braden felt sorry for her; where Kent was an outgoing performer Jacinta was an introvert.

Another round of clapping ensued, and Braden was surprised when Callie lifted his arm and she too stood. She grinned down at him and he grinned back.

'Well, I never,' he said.

'A bridesmaid, my dear, not a matron of honour,' she whispered.

'I'll bring you around,' he said.

Things had been tough lately. Since Nigel's meltdown, Callie had moved into the spare room, and he worried that it was the beginning of a division between them.

The new doctor, Harry Higgins, had assured him that giving Nigel time to adjust to Callie being their step-mum was wise. Braden was torn; he wanted the best for Nigel but there was no way he was going to let Callie go.

If he'd been a stronger man when Julia had died and kept the boys with him, and not relied on Sophie so much, maybe Nigel would have handled his grief easier.

'Patience, my darling.' Callie's lips brushing across his cheek made him feel a little better. 'I'll go and order for us. You grab yourself another beer.'

At least Callie had agreed to stay in a room with him at the pub tonight; the boys were sleeping over at the Malone house under Ruth's care.

'The usual steak with mushroom sauce?' she asked. 'And garlic bread?'

'You know me well.'

'I do.' She dropped another kiss on the top of his head and he squeezed her hand as it rested on his shoulder.

Braden watched as she walked across to the bar, stopping to chat with several people as she passed their tables. He shook his head with a grin. Callie had only been here a short while and she had made many friends. A surge of love rose in his chest and he vowed he would fight to keep her with him for the rest of his life.

As Callie left the table closest to the bar and walked across to the counter with Sophie, Braden's attention was taken by a sudden movement across the table. Kent half-rose in his chair, his face leached of all colour as he stared at the doorway that led out to the street.

'What the . . .' he exclaimed.

# Chapter 2

*Harry*

Harry Higgins's day had not been the easy one he'd anticipated. But he'd survived and he now sat at the end of the bar of the busy pub in Augathella, waiting for his drink.

*The first of two only,* he told himself.

Keeping his head down, Harry tried to avoid engaging with anyone. He had considered buying a bottle of scotch and taking it home to his small residence at the back of the surgery, but that was too risky. Plus, he didn't want the word to get around that he was a drinker.

*Not that he was. Not anymore.*

Harry enjoyed being in Augathella, and although he'd been welcomed by the community in the month since his arrival, he preferred to remain fairly aloof. He'd learned over the years not to get involved with patients on a personal level, especially in small towns. Jenny had told him more than once that he came across as a snob, but that didn't bother him. As the local doctor, he needed to keep that distance, although he had been invited and accepted some invitations out to local stations.

He didn't mind weekend duty at the small Augathella hospital—this was his third—he had foolishly expected Saturday to be a quiet day. He'd packed his lunch at seven and picked up a book that had just arrived in the post—time travel fiction, not a medical text. As he sat in the back courtyard of the hospital in the warm winter sun he anticipated an easy day, without having to do too much in the emergency department. This small town would suit him very well for the remainder of his medical career.

*What a cop-out.*

He blocked Jenny's voice from his mind. The voice that never left him. Even though she had.

So much for his quiet day; today had been a shocker. On his last Saturday shift, Harry's only patient was a local farmer who'd come off his horse and suffered a slight concussion. Today he had expected much the same.

'My wife insisted on bringing me to the hospital,' Craig Wilson had said. 'Between you and me, doc, it was only so she could have a coffee in town. I've had worse falls than this one in my time on the land.' He shook his head and grinned. 'I needed some stuff at the rural store anyway, so I gave in. She's down at the café and I'm off to the store when you give me the all-clear.'

They'd had a long chat and Harry had learned more about the district. Then when Craig was collected by his wife, Harry spent the rest of the day in the sun reading the first book in the series that took him to a place where there was no sadness and no regrets.

Yes, this small country town would do him very well. Today he'd expected to see maybe the odd bike or skateboard accident patch-up, and maybe the occasional chest pain.

But it was not to be.

Every child who attended the local daycare centre had picked up and carried home a gastro bug, sharing it with the rest of their family. Harry spent the day dealing with a dozen vomiting families. Bec Hunter, the sole nurse on duty had been a great help as Harry had admitted one mother and child and provided advice to the others. The pharmacy had stayed open all day on his request to dispense oral rehydration solutions. He'd gone home at four and soaked in a long hot shower to chase away the smell. So, when he'd arrived at the pub and the friendly barman asked him what his drink of choice was, he had no hesitation in ordering a double scotch on the rocks. After the day he'd had, he deserved it.

*Selfish git,* Jenny said. *That was not a bad day, Harry. A few kids with diarrhoea. What have you become?*

The pub was crowded tonight, and he decided next time he went to Charleville, he *would* get a bottle for home. He'd walked up from the residence about three streets away, surprised to see so many cars parked in the usually quiet town. As the winter approached, the town seemed to get busier. The surgery had been hectic through the week too, but Harry liked that. A busy day, no time to think.

Some of his patients were the grey nomies who travelled through the district in their caravans. They called in to get prescriptions renewed and have the odd ailment checked out. But the majority of his patients were those who lived on outlying stations; when he'd applied for the position Harry hadn't realised what a huge area this town serviced.

He'd assumed it was a tiny town where he could just bury himself away, see some patients, read lots of books and live the quiet life he yearned for. He'd looked for a while before choosing Augathella; he'd been offered a job in a private hospital in Darwin, but he'd said no to that one as soon as he got the call.

After interviews in a few larger centres: Longreach, Mount Isa and Cloncurry, he'd kept looking.

*Too big. Too many memories.*

Then he'd seen the job here.

*Harry,* Jenny sighed in his head.

'Bugger off, Jenny,' Harry muttered.

'Sorry, what was that, doc? Another drink?' The barman leaned over the bar.

'Sorry, just talking to myself,' he said as heat ran up his neck.

He didn't want to be known as a drunk or an eccentric so for a few minutes Harry made an effort to converse with the barman, who introduced himself as Dave.

'Busy night tonight, doc.' Dave nodded towards a large table where over a dozen people were chatting and laughing. 'Braden Cartwright's family and friends. He's one of our most respected cattlemen. A good bloke and a good boss. I've done some work out on his station. He's done it tough though. It's good to see him out and about.'

Harry nodded and looked over at the happy group. He knew Braden and his partner, Callie. He knew that Braden had lost his wife a few years back and that his kids were still grieving. Harry had been impressed with Callie when he'd had dinner out there a couple of weeks ago; she'd been sensible and down to earth as they'd chatted about young Nigel when they came into the surgery last week. He'd taken particular notice of the Cartwright fellow too. A typical Aussie bloke, his grief was obviously buried deep, and perhaps unacknowledged. Maybe he'd catch up with him next time he brought Nigel in, and talk to Braden about how he was coping. He could point him in the right direction.

*Huh, can you really, Harry? Jenny said.*

Harry ignored her persistent voice and nodded at Dave. 'Yep, nice bloke. Everyone I've met so far has been. I think this town is going to suit me very well.'

Dave grinned at him and left him to his whisky as he went to serve at the other end of the bar.

Harry relaxed as the spirit wended its warm way through his veins. Yes, Augathella was going to suit him very well. He savoured the smooth slip of the Glenfiddich down his throat and shut his mind to Jenny and his memories. He half-turned on the bar stool and focused on the activity in the room around him.

The bistro was full tonight and several groups had spilled out into the bar area; he'd already recognised many of the people who were there and had acknowledged some greetings, but there were quite a few tourists here tonight as well.

Braden Cartwright sat at the head of the large table, but there was no sign of the three Cartwright boys. But Harry had noticed a group of children playing out on the lawn at the back of the pub. It would be helpful to see how young Nigel interacted with other children.

*Poor little fellow*. Harry hoped his talk to the young boy had helped him sort out his thoughts and feelings a little. He also hoped that they'd kept the appointment the receptionist had made with the child psychologist. It was one of the saddest cases he'd seen. Nigel had opened up and his grief and anger had spilled out as soon as his father had left them alone.

Harry hadn't shared with Braden a lot of what Nigel had told him; he'd talked generally about what Nigel needed. Braden and Callie had been receptive and agreed to see the child psychologist in Charleville the same week. He just hoped they hadn't changed their minds.

Hopefully, he'd see a gradual improvement in Nigel when he came in next week. Harry made a mental note to speak to Braden alone too.

He lifted his head and scanned the room. There was little risk of anyone waylaying him for a conversation. The only other lone drinker was head down at the end of the bar and hadn't even looked at him. Everyone was immersed in conversation. Laughter filled the large area and for a while, Harry's spirits lifted.

A shadow crossed the window and his gaze settled on a tall, attractive woman who paused in the double doorway that led onto the footpath. His curiosity was piqued as she looked around the room with a determined expression. Extremely well dressed in a dark blue suit, with high-heeled shoes, and carrying a large leather bag, she looked very much out of place in this casual country pub.

Her long hair was loose and when she turned to look outside, as though she was having second thoughts about coming inside, the light caught the gold rim on her sunglasses. It matched the gold chain around her neck.

*Yes, certainly out of place here.*

He watched unashamedly as the woman took a deep breath and lifted her fingers in a beckoning gesture. To his surprise, Braden Cartwright stood and crossed the room. Her face was set in an expressionless mask as Braden walked towards her.

Harry glanced back at the table and the young woman across from Braden looked up as the man beside her touched her arm, and her face lost its colour.

*What was going on?*

No one else seemed to be taking any notice, but the couple at Braden's table didn't take their eyes off him as he reached the tall woman.

Something wasn't quite right here, Harry thought. He knew he wasn't good socially, but he was intuitive. Their reactions were strange and despite the happy conversations around him, Harry could sense the level of tension in the air.

He waited as Braden spoke to the woman for a minute or so. She nodded at him and Braden took her arm, a nervous tic jumping in his cheek. The woman shook her head and pointed to the table he had left. Harry held his breath as they turned and Braden led the woman to their table just as Callie came back from the bistro counter.

# Chapter 3

Laura Adnum had driven around the small town centre three times before she found a parking space. Her hands gripped the steering wheel of the luxury hire car; she'd wanted to make a good impression but had soon discovered that a luxury sedan wasn't the right vehicle for the conditions out here.

And out here was so much further than she'd imagined. Used to driving on the green grass-edged roads of home, entering the outback had been a tremendous shock. Okay, she'd seen photos and watched videos of the remoter parts of Australia, but the heat and the dryness that had met her as she stepped from the car today had shocked her.

*And this was winter?*

But she'd soldiered on; she had to. On the dirt road out to the Cartwright station, she'd almost turned back, but had continued; Laura wanted to see how they actually were living.

She didn't want to give him time to make it look like they were living the life of a happy family. She wanted to see how things really were—not a sanitised version. She knew from Julia what a hard man he was, and she wanted to take Braden Cartwright by surprise. So, she hadn't told Braden she was coming to visit.

Then when she'd got there, there had been no one home. An old fellow came out of one of the small huts and told her that Braden and his wife were at the pub in town.

That'd be right, she thought. This time of night, the boys should be having dinner and getting ready to go to bed, not stuck in a hotel while their father and his new *wife* drank. So, she turned around and navigated that horrendous road of red, soft dirt back to town.

After Laura parked the car, she checked her hair and makeup in the small mirror behind the sun visor and reapplied her pink lipstick. If she looked good, she would be more confident, and the nerves would stay away.

As she climbed out of the car, she took herself to task.

*Why should I be nervous?*

She'd come here with a purpose. Letting her temper build and increase her confidence even more, she strode towards the hotel.

Loud music from the bar mixed with voices and laughter, and suddenly Laura felt out of her depth. Her body sagged as tiredness tugged at her determination and she wondered if she should just find a motel and confront Braden when she felt stronger. The early start at Tauranga yesterday, the drive to Auckland, followed by a three-hour flight and then a day and a half of driving on unfamiliar outback roads had taken a toll on her energy.

No. She would not give in. Her nephews' safety and happiness were at risk here.

Laura stood at the door of the hotel and fought the fear rising in her throat. She smoothed trembling hands down the front of her linen suit and took a deep breath.

Focus on what the psychologist said.

*Focus.*

*I can do this.* With another deep breath, she evened her breathing.

'You right there, love?' A wavering voice came from behind her.

Laura jumped and concentrated on staying calm. Turning slowly, she turned to look at the elderly man sitting at a table on the footpath, a glass of beer in his hand.

'You're shaking like a bloody leaf,' he said 'Are you waiting for someone, love? Have you been stood up? Fella's got rocks in his head if he's stood up a looker like you.'

Strangely his comment about her being a looker calmed her nerves. 'No, thank you, I'm fine. I was just deciding whether to go in and have dinner.' Laura summoned up a smile.

'You should then. Sean puts on a great feed here, love.' He tapped his nose with his free hand.

'Plus, he's a good bloke. Got a bit of a roving eye, but he makes sure I get a meal out here every night.'

'It does smell delicious.' Her hands had stopped shaking.

'You won't get a better feed this side of the black stump,' he said.

Even though she had no idea what he was talking about, she nodded. 'In that case, I will have to try the meal here.'

'Where are you from, love? You've got a strange twang in your voice.'

Laura hesitated, not wanting to share anything about herself until she had got the lay of the situation here in Augathella. 'I'm just visiting the district,' she said.

'Well, you've picked the best town to visit along with good grub here in the pub.'

Laura couldn't help her smile widening. 'You're a very good advocate for your town.'

The old fellow who was in need of a shave tipped his head to the side and grinned at her. 'Don't assume too much. That's a good way to be. You tell me where you're from, love, and I'll tell you whether I'm a local here or not. I could be pulling your leg, you know.'

'I'm a Kiwi, and it's been nice chatting to you.'

'Likewise. I'm Reg. I like to have a chat with the pub customers. A man learns a lot that way.'

With a nod, Laura left the man to his beer and stepped inside the door before her courage deserted her.

She stood straight and stepped into a wall of noise. Her eyes scanned the room; everyone seemed to be talking at once and, combined with the loud music, the sound made her head spin. Her eyes narrowed as she spotted her brother-in-law at the head of a long table. She'd never met him but had seen him in many of the family photos that Julia had emailed every week. A pretty young woman leaned over and dropped a kiss on his head and walked across to the counter.

*The new wife?*

How dare he? Braden hadn't communicated with her once since his initial phone call telling her that Julia was dead. Grief stuck in her throat as she remembered that afternoon. Laura had grasped her stomach and dropped to her knees keening with grief. After that, it had been his sister, Sophie, who had called to tell her of the funeral arrangements. Laura would never forgive herself for not coming then, but she hadn't been able to travel. She'd begged the doctor but both he and Brett had convinced her it was too risky.

'Besides, sweetheart, she won't even know you're not there. You have to accept that your sister is gone.' Brett always had been the sensible one.

The voice of reason, whether she agreed or not. Now it was time for her to be strong and sensible.

Laura quickly looked around, but there was no sign of her three nephews. As she fixed her gaze on Braden, he looked up and she pinned her gaze on him. She saw the moment he recognised her, and the shock that crossed his face.

His discomfort gave her great satisfaction; he could suffer too. He stood and as he made his way across the room her heart thudded erratically. She focused on his face, willing herself to calm down. Harsh words would not gain her any leeway.

Laura knew what she wanted, and she knew what she had to do. It was what Julia would have wanted.

\*\*\*

When Braden had first seen the woman at the door his breath hitched and it seemed as though his heart literally missed a beat. Sophie reached across the table to him, her expression reflecting his shock.

*Julia?*

His vision blurred and he struggled to take a breath.

And then sense kicked in. Julia was in the local cemetery, and this woman was a lot taller than his wife had been. But the shock of seeing a face almost identical to hers had him standing without even thinking about it.

He gripped the back of his chair and stared at her. Without thinking, he walked slowly across to the door.

'Hello, Braden.' Her tone was cold and her accent plummy, and he suddenly realised who it was.

'Laura?' he said slowly.

'Yes, Braden. I guess it's a shock you certainly didn't want to have. It looks like all I've heard is true. You and your new woman are out drinking and having a party while those three motherless boys are where?' She looked around. 'Out in the beer garden? Or home alone? Nothing would surprise me from you.'

'All you've heard?'

'Yes.'

Braden took her arm and tried to lead her outside before she made a scene.

She shook her head and moved away from him.

'No, you're not dragging me outside where you can make your paltry excuses. I'd like to meet your new wife.' She paused, and as she put a manicured finger to pink-painted lips, her voice held venom. 'Now I wonder what her relationship would be to me? Sister-in-law once removed? I'm sure there's some sort of tag.'

'I do not have a new wife, Laura. Not that that is really any of your business.' A chill ran through

Braden and he glanced over to Callie automatically. She was still at the counter beside Jacinta ordering their meals.

'Oh, but it is, Braden. I carry some responsibility for my sister's three boys. I'm here to see whether you are a suitable father. Or not. And if not, I will deal with it. Others may not be game to confront you, but I have no reason to fear you. I can assure you of that. The boys' welfare is all I care about.'

Braden struggled to reply. Julia had always told him what a loose cannon his sister-in-law was, and despite being married to Julia for almost seven years, he'd never once met Laura Adnum. As far as he'd known she'd still lived in the UK. Then he remembered Sophie had tracked her down to New Zealand.

'Suitable?' he finally choked out.

'Yes, suitable.'

'This is not the place to have such a ridiculous discussion,' he replied. 'Please calm down and we'll have a rational conversation later.'

Not that he wanted to have any conversation with her. *What on earth was she doing here in Augathella?*

'Very well. That will be suitable.'

He stared at her, as he felt a tic pulsing in his cheek.

'Now are you going to invite me to join your friends?' she asked.

# Chapter 4

Braden took Laura's arm and steered her through the bar area, across to the table at the far side of the room where his group was sitting. He stared ahead and ignored the curious glances and shocked faces of locals. Sophie watched them every step of the way, her face still pale. Just before they reached the table, Callie turned from the bistro counter and headed back to the table. Braden caught her eye and she raised her eyebrows as she looked at the woman beside him. As his eyes had a few minutes before, Callie's widened too and her mouth dropped open. She'd seen enough photos of Julia in the house to pick the resemblance and wonder what the hell was going on.

Braden shook his head slowly and smiled at her, giving her a nod to try and let her know that everything was okay.

*Not that it really was okay.*

He couldn't believe that Laura had turned up here and what ridiculous things she had to say. A ripple of guilt ran through Braden wondering if she knew—and if she did how she'd found out—that his boys had lived with Sophie while he'd got his act together after Julia's accident.

*For almost two years?* He could predict her sarcastic comment if she knew.

He was recovered now and he didn't need any ex-sister-in-law telling him what to do.

Julia had never wanted to visit her sister as they had had a falling out a couple of years before Braden had met Julia. Laura was full of belligerence, and it appeared she was here to make trouble.

'She's bossy, thinks she is always right, and I don't care if I never see her again.'

Despite her harsh words, Braden knew that Julia had sent photos of the boys and that she and Laura had emailed each other frequently. He frowned. He did recall Julia saying something about her emigrating to New Zealand where her husband had come from.

Why she'd chosen to turn up now though, and not three years ago was beyond him.

At the moment, with the way Nigel was and with Callie appearing to have second thoughts about their marriage, Laura Adnum was the last visitor they wanted. The last person he needed to interfere in his life. To interfere in *their* lives.

As they approached the table, Braden focused on staying calm

They reached the table at the same time Callie did and Braden turned to her, speaking before Laura could make a scene. He was sure that was what she intended, and he was determined not to give her the chance.

He took Callie's hand. 'Callie, this is Laura. Laura, this is Callie Young, my fiancée.' He stared at Laura, challenging her with his eyes.

Callie didn't give her a chance to say anything rude. She smiled sweetly. 'Hello, Laura, how wonderful to meet you. Welcome to Augathella.'

Laura's voice was low and he could tell her smile was forced. 'Hello, Callie. I'm Braden's sister-in-law, and the boys' aunt.'

'Yes. I recognised you. We weren't expecting you to visit. Did you try to call?'

'No, I—' Before she could finish, Sophie had jumped to her feet. 'Hello, Laura. I'm Braden's sister, Sophie. The boys' other aunt.'

Laura turned and it was hard to read her expression. 'Hello, Sophie. Julia told me a lot about you. It's good to finally meet you.' Tears glistened in her eyes as she mentioned Julia, and Braden remembered it had been Sophie who had made the call the day of the accident.

Kent stood and moved across next to Sophie as she wiped her eyes.

'This is Kent,' Braden said. 'Sophie's partner.'

Kent moved the chairs along and went across and collected a spare one from the empty table under the window. 'Have a seat, Laura, and we'll introduce you to the rest of this lot.'

There was a shuffling of seats and bodies as they made room for the extra chair.

'What would like to drink, Laura?' Braden kept his voice even and polite, despite the anger churning in him.

'A soda water would be fine.'

'We've all ordered our meals,' Sophie said. 'Would you like to see the menu and Braden can order for you while he's at the bar?'

Laura waved an elegant hand, and Braden couldn't help comparing it to the work-roughened hands of her sister. Julia had always been out on the station with her horses and had had no time—nor desire—for manicures. After Braden and the boys, her horses had been her love.

'A salad would be fine, thank you.' Laura opened her small bag. 'Let me give you my card.'

Braden shook his head. 'Don't be silly. You're our guest.'

*Uninvited guest* went unspoken.

He nodded and went across to the bar and stood waiting to be served.

'Hello, Braden,' a quiet, deep voice said beside him.

Pulled out of his not-so-pleasant thoughts, Braden turned to see the new doctor observing him. 'Hello, Dr Higgins,' he said.

'Harry, please. It's Saturday night at the pub. No need for ceremony.'

'Hello, Harry,' he said. 'Good to see you out and about. It's busy in here tonight.'

'Yes, I was just thinking about ordering some dinner and heading home.'

Braden narrowed his eyes as he had a brainwave. 'Why don't you join us? Our table's just ordered. Better than eating alone.'

*And I'll sit him beside the witch,* he thought. Maybe she'd be less likely to perform with the local doctor at the table.

'No. It looks like you've got a big enough group, already.'

'I insist. I'm about to order another meal, so let me order for you at the same time.'

Dave was standing at the bar listening unashamedly. Braden flicked him a frown, but he didn't get it.

'Steak and veg for you, doc?' Dave said moving back to the till. 'Same as every night? I'll add it to Braden's order.'

'And a salad and a soda water, please, Dave,' Braden added. 'Now come on, Harry, I'll introduce you to a few more of the locals.' He handed his credit card over as Dave rang up the orders and then poured a middy of soda water from the post-mix machine.

'Another scotch, doc?' he asked as he handed it over to Braden.

'No, thank, you,' Harry said. 'This will do me for the night.' He turned to Braden. 'I don't want to intrude.'

'Mate, this is the Augathella pub. No such thing as intruding.' He sensed the doc's reluctance and paused. 'And you can do me a favour. We've had an unexpected visitor and if you could keep her entertained for a while, I'll be forever grateful.'

'I can do that. I did see the young woman arrive.'

Braden tensed as he spoke. 'It's my sister-in-law. We've never met before and between you and me, I'm a bit worried about why she's turned up.'

'You've never met?' Harry frowned.

'No. She couldn't get to our wedding or Julia's funeral. We always planned to visit her, but never got there.'

'I'm happy to chat with her. It doesn't happen often, but I can be sociable when necessary.' Harry's voice was gruff, but he grinned at Braden.

'I'll owe you one, doc. And please don't think that's why I asked you. I thought it was a good chance for you to meet some more of the townsfolk.

They're a good bunch of people. A healthy young mob, so I doubt if you've encountered any of them at the surgery.'

They stood at the table and after he'd introduced Harry to the group, Kent began to chat with him. Braden tried to catch Callie's eye but to no avail. He hurried across the room to get a chair for Harry.

'Harry, grab a seat,' he said after he'd put it beside Laura.

Braden waited to get Callie's attention, but she and Laura were deep in conversation.

Braden's skin crawled with unease.

*What was Laura up to?*

# Chapter 5

*Harry*

Despite his reluctance to join the group for dinner, Harry was surprised to find himself having an enjoyable time. Somehow Dave had decided he needed another drink and Braden returned from the bar with another Scotch when their meals were brought to the table.

'It's only a single nip,' he said as he placed the glass in front of Harry. 'I heard you tell Kent you were on duty at the hospital tomorrow.'

'Thank you.' Harry nodded his appreciation.

'You're a doctor?' the woman beside him—Braden's sister-in-law— asked.

Harry hadn't been introduced to her as she'd been deep in conversation with Callie when he'd met the rest of the group. He held his hand out. 'Dr Harry Higgins, ma'am, and you are?'

'I'm Laura Adnum.'

'Nice to meet you, Laura. I saw you arrive and you looked rather lost. You're new in town too?'

'I'm visiting,' she said. 'Braden's wife was my sister.'

'I'm sorry for your loss. I know it's been a while, but grief never leaves us, does it?'

She lifted her head and held his gaze, and the sadness in her dark eyes resonated with him, sparking unwanted memories.

'No. No, it doesn't. How did you know about Julia? I mean you said you're new in town. Has it been the subject of discussion at the pub? Are locals talking about Braden remarrying?'

Harry hesitated. He couldn't say that Nigel was a patient. 'One of the things about small towns, and settling into a new place, the locals like to let you know the background so you don't put a foot wrong, or say the wrong thing.'

*That would have to suffice*, he thought.

'Yes, I guess I do know that. I lived in a small town once. Nothing was private there.'

Harry was surprised at the bitterness in her voice. 'But small towns certainly have their positives. I have always found that the community rallies when help is needed. That's why I always choose to work in places like that,' he said.

*Well,* he thought, *that's partly the truth.*

'So, tell me, Laura. Where is home for you?'

Again, sadness crossed her face as she gave a small shrug.

'That's a bit hard to answer. I've just sold my house and left my job, so I'm not sure where I'll end up.'

'But that is a Kiwi or a British accent if I'm correct. Is that where your home is . . . or was?'

She nodded. 'Yes, New Zealand in recent years. I haven't decided where I'm going to settle. It depends on what I find here.'

*A strange way to put it,* Harry thought. *What was she expecting to find?*

'A very pretty place. I worked in Christchurch after the earthquake,' he said, not showing his uncertainty. 'I was with one of the Australian medical teams.'

'I was in the north,' she said. 'I haven't been to the South Island since before the earthquake.

'And will you settle back there, or are you here to look at moving to Australia?'

Another small shrug, and a gentle sigh. 'That's a hard question to answer, Harry. I really don't know at the moment. Like I said, depends what I find.'

'It's good to have choices.'

'Is it? I think I'd rather everything be the same as it always was,' was her enigmatic answer.

A tap on his shoulder made him jump. 'Steak and veg for you, doc?' the waitress asked.

'Yes, thank you.' When Harry turned back to Laura her attention was on the bowl of salad in front of her. He turned his attention to his meal and ignored his glass of scotch. Conversations at the table quietened as the group ate, and the single discussion turned to the upcoming performing arts festival in Charleville.

Kent Mason and Ben Riley, who Harry had met for the first time tonight, were apparently on the committee and were drumming up interest.

'It'll be a fabulous event,' Kent said. 'Do you reckon you can get the kids at school interested, Jacinta?'

'What sort of activities?' the young woman called Jacinta, asked. 'Is it like an eisteddfod?'

'Sort of. There are musical items, speech and drama, choirs, dance, and even some comedy sketches. Open to all ages. Ben's been doing the rounds of the aged care facilities in Augathella and Morven, and I'm going to Charleville after the cattle have gone this week.'

Jacinta and Callie both looked at each other and chuckled. They both spoke at the same time and Harry noticed Laura sit up and take notice.

'Rory,' they both said together.

'He's the class clown,' Jacinta continued. 'I think we could channel that into something suitable.'

'Rory?' Laura said. 'Is that Julia's Rory?'

The long silence was a bit strained until Braden filled it. 'Yes. *Our* Rory. He's always been a little comedian.'

Sophie jumped in. 'When he lived with . . . after Julia . . . I mean, when he lived with me, he was always dressing up and performing. He's got talent.' Harry noticed the nervous glance she sent in Laura's direction, and he realised that she must be Braden's sister. The aunt the three boys had lived with after their mother died. Nigel had seemed to be close to his Aunty Sophie.

'Julia loved theatre when she was in her teens,' Laura said quietly. 'He must take after her.'

'He does,' Braden said quietly. 'In many ways.'

'I'm looking forward to meeting my nephews,' she said, lifting her chin.

'Are you staying in town?' Braden asked. 'We'll have to organise something tomorrow. We'll all be in town tomorrow because we're staying in tonight.'

Harry looked around the table. Everyone was quiet, obviously sensing the tension at the table.

'Callie's invited me to stay at Kilcoy Station,' Laura said. 'And I've accepted.'

Harry was taken aback by Braden's dark look at Callie as he ignored Laura's statement. As much as Laura seemed to be a pleasant woman, Harry was surprised by her glare as she turned to Braden.

There was a strange undercurrent running through their conversation.

'Do you have a vehicle, Laura?' Harry asked. He was pleased he was here to defuse the tension a little bit.

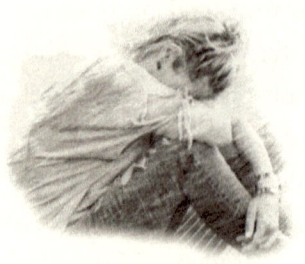

# Chapter 6

*Callie*

Callie froze as Braden stiffened beside her. She looked up at him and noticed a nerve jumping in his cheek. The one that flickered when he was upset. It wasn't the right time to ask him—in front of Laura—what had upset him, but from the look on his face, and the way he moved away from her, she knew he wasn't happy with her.

His voice was clipped as he replied. 'Well, that will make things easy, then. How long are you here for, Laura?'

Callie flinched. That had sounded very rude, and distinctly unwelcoming. For some reason, Braden didn't like his sister-in-law. But she was family to the boys, he had to understand that. Not having any family of her own heightened Callie's sensitivity to Laura's right to spend time with her nephews. But it was clear that Braden had a problem with that, and Callie was disappointed with his reaction.

Laura lifted her head and stared at Braden. 'For as long as it takes.'

Callie couldn't help herself. 'As what takes?'

'To get to know my nephews and see how happy they are.' Laura's voice was cold and the others at the table turned away and began to talk quietly to give them privacy.

Except for Sophie who was staring at Laura. Sophie's face was flushed, and she looked upset.

And so did Fallon. She looked to be in pain.

Callie frowned as Fallon grabbed her stomach and reached out for Jon.

Ignoring Braden and Laura, Callie jumped to her feet and hurried around the table. She crouched down beside Fallon.

'Are you okay?'

Fallon shook her head. 'No. My back has been aching on and off all day, and I just had the most dreadful cramp in my stomach.' Her face flushed a dark pink. 'And now I'm sitting in a wet pool. Something's happened.'

Jon jumped up and put his arms around her. 'My God, we'd better get you to the hospital.'

'No. Ssh,' Fallon hissed. 'I'm not getting up. I'm too embarrassed. I'm all wet.'

'There's nothing to be embarrassed about, Fallon,' Callie said.

'There is. I'm not walking out of here with soaking wet maternity jeans.'

'So, what are you going to do? Have our baby in the bar of the hotel?' Jon's voice got the attention of the whole table.

'Duh, no. I'm not due for four weeks.' Fallon snapped and then let out a yelp and grabbed Jon's arm. 'Oh, my stomach's cramping again. I must have eaten something off.'

Callie looked up as someone walked around and stood behind her.

'Fallon?' Dr Harry's voice was calm. 'I don't think it's anything you've eaten. I think your baby's decided to come a little bit early.' He turned to Jon. Do you want me to get the ambulance, or can you drive her to the hospital?'

'I'll take her right now. Callie, can you help me?'

Fallon shook her head and leaned forward. 'No, Callie, can you go and tell Mum, please? She's going to be my support person. But you come back too. I need you to look after Mum. I know what she'll be like.' Callie grinned. It was so typical of Fallon to be organised and worry about everyone else.

Dr Harry turned to Jon. 'I'm sure you've got plenty of help here. I'll walk down to the hospital and call the midwife.'

'No,' Fallon ground out between clenched teeth. 'I saw Helen at the clinic yesterday and she told me not to have the baby this weekend because she was going to Mitchell to see her daughter.'

'I'll call Jenna,' Harry said.

Callie shook her head. 'She's gone to Longreach for a netball tournament.'

'Well, Fallon, it looks like you're stuck with me.'

Callie frowned as she heard the slight wobble in the doctor's voice.

By now, the whole group was transfixed by the tableau unfolding in front of them. Callie looked at Braden, and then at Sophie. Jacinta and Amelia sat there quietly looking unsure.

Laura stood. 'I'm a qualified midwife,' she said. 'I'm not sure what the protocols are, but I can help if you need me.'

'Thank you, Laura. Perhaps you could come to the hospital and be on standby? A couple of the nurses who were on duty today have, I believe, done their training, but I'll have to get them to come in. They had a big day today, but I'm sure we can get someone.'

Braden glanced at Callie, but his face was closed. 'I'll help Jon get Fallon into the car. You go down to the Malones and get Ruth. Wait with the boys until I come back.'

*No please, no thank you, no nothing.* For the first time since she and Braden had been together,

Callie felt like the hired help. The nanny who'd come from Brisbane. The nanny who at this very minute could very easily go back to her house on the river in Brisbane without a second thought.

Callie's throat clogged but she refused to let Braden—or anyone else for that matter—see she was upset. Sophie shot her a sympathetic glance. She'd picked up on her brother's tone.

'Laura?' Braden's voice was full of authority. 'I'll tell Dave that you can have our room here for the night. Callie and I will stay at the Malones with the boys.'

*And we'll stay in separate rooms if we do,* Callie thought as her temper flared.

Fallon gave another yelp and grabbed for Callie. 'Will you come with me now, Cal?' she asked, her voice shaking. 'Stay with me?'

'Braden, can you go down and tell Ruth after you leave the hospital? Fallon wants me to stay with her now.' Callie stared at him and waited for him to disagree.

Sophie stood and came around to the side of the table where Callie and Fallon were. 'You go now, Braden,' she said. 'Kent and I can help out here if we're needed.'

Braden nodded but didn't speak. 'I'll help Jon get her to the ute and then I'll go and get Ruth.'

Callie was surprised when she turned and intercepted the look that Laura gave Braden. There was something about this woman that seemed out of kilter.

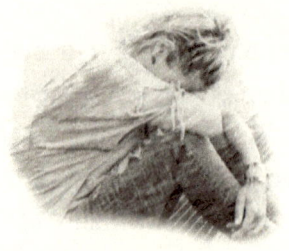

# Chapter 7

*Laura*

Laura waited quietly as Fallon's husband and Braden helped Fallon stand, and then supported her out across the room to the door. Sophie and Callie walked behind them, shielding Fallon from the view of the diners in the bistro as they walked through. A buzz of interested conversation and the occasional 'Good luck, Fallon,' followed them.

Kent had taken the keys from Jon and already brought a car around. A bright red vintage utility vehicle was now parked outside the door and only a couple of minutes passed before they had Fallon in the car and were headed off to the hospital, which from all accounts was only a couple of blocks away.

The friendship among the group was obviously strong, and Laura was beginning to feel a bit like an outsider.

*Which I am,* she told herself. For a brief moment, she regretted being so hard on Braden, and then she remembered why she was here.

*Don't soften. I'm here for the boys. No one else.*

She jumped as a warm hand lightly touched her wrist.

'Thank you, Laura. I appreciate your offer of help. Where will I find you?' Harry asked. He'd stepped outside with his phone for a moment. 'And I guess I should ask do you have a working visa?'

'I do have copies of my certificates with me and I'm fine to work. Kiwis don't need a visa to work in Australia.'

'Ah, that's excellent. I wasn't aware of that. I have a feeling I may have to take you up on your offer. I've made a couple of quick calls and both the nurses who were on today have already come down with that stomach bug.'

'I'm happy to help any way I can.'

'That's excellent. May I have your phone number?'

'Sure.' Laura reached into her bag for a pen. 'But I guess I can just wait here in the bar.'

'Didn't Braden say that you could have their room?'

'Yes, but I'm not comfortable with that. I don't know them well enough to just go up and take that over.'

'I'm sure there will be other rooms available. Most of the tourists in here for dinner tonight will have their caravans.'

Laura nodded. 'I'll go and ask and see if I can get a room of my own. It looks like I won't be out at the station until at least tomorrow.'

Harry's look was shrewd. 'Are you sure you want to stay out there? It's a long way out of town, I believe.'

'Yes, it is. I drove out there this afternoon. Foolishly, I was expecting them to be home.'

'And you didn't tell them you were coming? I did get the impression Braden was surprised to see you.'

'No, I didn't. I wanted my visit to be a surprise.'

Again, the doctor's look was penetrating, and Laura sensed that he'd picked up on her tone. It wasn't meant as a nice surprise.

She smiled; she didn't want to get the doctor offside. She knew she had a problem with men; Brett had often told her she was rude. If she needed help once she found out what was going on with the boys, perhaps Dr Harry might be a good ally. The rest of their friends here tonight seemed very tight.

'You'd better get going. I'll wait for your call,' Laura said as she wrote her mobile number on a coaster and handed it to him.

The doctor's grin was cheeky, and Laura realised he was younger than she had first thought. The salt and pepper hair belied his age. She guessed he'd be around forty, five years older than she was.

'Long time since I've had a woman's number on a beer coaster.' His voice was self-deprecating.

Heat ran up into Laura's cheeks. 'Call me. If you need help with the *delivery*.'

'I will. I'll head off to the hospital now and I'll give you a call either way in half an hour or so to let you know how it's going.' Harry stood beside her and reached out and took her hand. 'It's been lovely to meet you, Laura, and I do appreciate very much your offer of help.'

'It's certainly been an eventful evening,' she said.

He looked at her quizzically but she didn't say what she was thinking. She'd only met this man an hour or so ago and even though she felt as though she could trust him, she didn't want to disclose her real purpose for being in Augathella.

But she would keep him onside.

She squeezed his hand and was gratified to see warmth flare in his deep blue eyes.

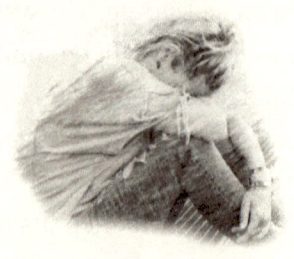

# Chapter 8

*Braden*

'I'll go straight away,' Ruth said to Braden, grabbing her keys from the cupboard beside the kitchen door. 'The boys are all asleep. They had a big afternoon, and it was a bit chilly outside so we had an early tea. Petie was the only one who wanted to watch television, but I read him a story and he was the first to go to sleep.'

'Thanks, Ruth. I appreciate you looking after them. When you get to the hospital can you tell Callie that I'll wait here with them until she comes back? Maybe someone could drop her back here? Or I can rouse the boys and pick her up, and then we can go home.'

'Of course. She can bring my car if she wants. And don't be silly. It's too late to wake those dear boys up and take them home. You and Callie stay the night here.' Ruth headed for the door and then stopped. 'Oh, dear, I'll need a cardigan, and I'd better ring my husband and tell him Fallon's having the baby. Jerry went back to Brisbane a couple of weeks ago, but I decided to stay here until the house sale goes through. I just had a feeling she'd go early.'

Ruth hurried back down the hall and came back with a cardigan around her shoulders. 'Please don't wake the boys up. I can put some clean sheets on the bed in the third bedroom for you and Callie.'

Braden smiled and put his hands on Ruth's shoulders and steered her to the door. 'Ruth, go. Or you might miss the birth of your grandchild.'

'Oh goodness me. Is it that close?' She was out the door in seconds, and as Braden watched the car back down the driveway, Nigel called out.

He hurried down the hall and looked in each of the rooms until he found the room where the boys were sleeping.

Peti and Rory were sound asleep, but Nigel was sitting on the edge of the bed. His face lit up when he saw Braden at the door and he jumped up.

'Daddy! I want a drink and then I want to go home. The dogs will be missing us.'

Braden took his hand and led him out to the lounge room. 'I'll find you a drink and as soon as Callie gets here, we'll head back home. But mate, the dogs are fine. Charlie said he'd feed them and give them a run for us.'

As much as Braden appreciated Ruth's offer, he wanted to get home. He didn't feel comfortable in someone else's house. The smell of mothballs was overpowering too. So much for the romantic night he'd planned for Callie. The distance between them had seemed to be growing since she'd moved out of their bedroom after Nigel's meltdown. He could understand that she wanted the best for the boys, but they couldn't let their relationship go.

Maybe it was him?

*Maybe I'm not good enough for her.*

He loved Callie, but he was beginning to worry that her feelings for him weren't as strong as his. Moving to Augathella had been a big change for her, but she seemed to enjoy the town and she'd made lots of friends. She and Fallon spoke on the phone every day. The primary school valued her work, and they'd asked her to stay full-time next term, but Callie had declined and said she was needed at the station.

And now Laura was here, and it appeared she wanted to cause trouble, although Braden had no idea why.

He needed to be in his own home, and he wanted Callie back there with him. That way they could talk more about their relationship; Braden was prepared to work as hard as he had to.

*I'm not going to lose her.* He knew he needed to reassure Callie that marrying him was right. For both of them.

He frowned. The way he'd spoken to Callie tonight when he was angry at Laura had been way out of line.

That woman had got under his skin. Her words had shocked him.

*What the heck was she doing here?*

Settling Nigel on the sofa, Braden went back to the kitchen and rummaged through the cupboards until he found the glasses. He filled it with water from the tap and went back to Nigel. 'Here you go, mate.'

Nigel drank it in one gulp and snuggled into Braden's side. 'Can I stay out here with you, Dad? That room smells funny.'

'You can.' Braden put his arm around Nigel and within minutes his son had gone back to sleep against him.

Braden moved carefully as he laid him on the sofa and covered him with a blanket. He pulled his phone out of his shirt pocket and walked back into the kitchen.

Was it too soon to text Callie? He wondered how it would be received. He'd been short with her, and hurt her feelings. His stomach clenched as he remembered the confusion in her eyes.

She'd welcomed Laura too readily, and he was cross that she'd done that before he'd had a chance to talk to her and tell her what his sister-in-law had said.

And how much her unannounced arrival had bothered him.

# Chapter 9

*Callie*

'Oh, Callie, what am I doing here?' Fallon moaned as she lay back in the soft chair and squeezed Callie's fingers. They were by themselves in the labour suite at the hospital. Dr Higgins had come in briefly, looking preoccupied and checked that Fallon was comfortable—she'd been between contractions then, so he'd smiled and left. Jon had gone out to park the car in the hospital car park.

'You'll be fine, love. Women have babies every day.' Callie was at a loss; this was way out of her experience.

'But it's too soon. Why did the doctor go? I can't remember what I have to do. Everything I learned in those classes has gone.' Fallon put her head back and closed her eyes as the next pain arrived. 'Cal, will you stay here? Please?' she muttered before she took a deep breath.

'I'm here. Jon will be back in a minute.' It was enough to talk Callie out of ever having children. Fallon was usually so strong, and she wasn't coping one little bit.

'No, stay here until the baby's born.'

'I will. If that's what you want.' Callie looked around as Jon came back into the room. 'Is there a nurse around?' she asked. When they'd passed the main nurses' station on the way in, and then followed the doctor's instructions to the labour suite, there hadn't been a sign of anyone. The lights were out in all the wards, and the silence was unnerving.

'No, there's no one around,' Jon said as he walked around to the other side of the bed and took Fallon's other hand. 'I'm back now, sweetheart.'

A loud siren sounded outside and then stopped abruptly. Fallon opened her eyes and tried to push herself up higher on the pillow. 'What's happening? Is there anyone here yet? Please get the nurse. I don't know what to do.'

'I'll go and find the doctor,' Jon said.

Fallon drew a deep breath and squeezed her eyes shut. 'Tell him to hurry, there's another one coming now.'

Callie and Jon exchanged a look of concern, and Jon took off. Fallon held Callie's hand so tightly she was sure it would bruise.

'I think you're supposed to breathe through it, aren't you?' Callie said, unsure of what to say and starting to feel a little panicked. She knew nothing about childbirth and babies, apart from what she'd seen at the movies.

Where the hell were the medical staff? Where was all the gear? This was supposed to be a labour ward. Her phone buzzed in her bag, but she ignored it. It would be Braden looking for her, but Fallon needed her more at the moment.

Relief filled Callie as footsteps sounded in the corridor outside, and she let out the breath she'd been holding when she spotted Fallon's mother looking into the room opposite.

'Ruth, we're in here,' she called.

'Mum,' Fallon groaned. 'It hurts.'

'It's okay, love,' Ruth said as she came in and crossed to the bed. 'It'll all be over before you know it.'

Callie leaned over Fallon. Her eyes were closed, her cheeks flushed, and perspiration dotted her brow. 'I'll go, Fallon, now that your mum's here.'

Fallon shook her head. 'Will you stay too, Cal? Please?'

'If you want me to. I'll just go and call Braden.'

'Okay. Don't be long. And can you find Jon, and the doctor or someone? Anyone?' Her voice rose on the last words.

'I'll be quick.' Callie scooted out the door, grabbing her phone from her bag on the way. Fallon was always calm and cool, so Callie knew that she was panicked too.

Where the heck had everyone gone?

She decided to find someone before she called Braden.

Hurrying down the corridor, she shook her head. Not that she'd ever been in hospitals much, but the ones in Brisbane where she'd visited friends over the years had always been busy and noisy. This building was quiet and empty.

On the way in, she'd spotted a sign that said Accident and Emergency, so she headed in that direction. Out the main door, down the steps and around the side of the building. To her relief, the lights were on. An ambulance was parked in the emergency bay, and she could see figures through the glass door. As she hurried across, Jon came around the other side of the building towards the entrance.

'I couldn't find the doc in the main part of the hospital, so I thought I'd try emergency. How is she?' he asked.

'A bit panicked. She sent me to look for you and the doctor.'

'I'm wondering if we should have driven to Charleville. We would have been almost there by now.'

Callie shook her head. 'She might have had the baby on the side of the highway. At least the doctor's here. Come, on let's go and see what's happening. She needs someone there now.'

Jon held the door open as they stepped into the emergency department. Three people waited on plastic chairs in the waiting room, and a nurse was speaking to someone at the counter. Jon's expression held frustration, as they stood waiting.

The door opened and they both gave a sigh of relief as Harry appeared, but their relief was short-lived.

'I'm sorry, Jon. I'll be there as soon as I can. We've had an emergency here. A car accident out on the highway. A caravan rolled. I'm just waiting for the emergency ambulance to arrive to take one patient down to Charleville. I can deal with his wife here, but I'll need to admit her. We're very short-staffed tonight, but I've called Laura and she should be here any minute to help with Fallon. Can you keep an eye out for her and show her to Fallon's room? As soon as the ambulance arrives, I'll come around.'

'Will do. I hope everyone is okay.' Jon nodded and before they reached the door Harry had disappeared again.

'You go back to Fallon and I'll wait out the front for Laura.' Callie smiled at Jon. 'And don't stress, everything will be fine and the baby will be here before you know it.' She injected brightness into her voice and tried not to let him see how worried she was.

'Thanks, Callie. I'm glad you're here. And I'm bloody pleased we were in town when the baby decided to make an early appearance.'

While Callie waited on the front steps for Laura to appear, she dialled Braden.

He picked up straight away. 'Callie, where are you?'

'I'm still at the hospital. Are the boys okay?'

'Sound asleep. We'll take them home when you get here. Are you coming now?'

'No. I could be a while. Fallon wants me to stay.'

There was silence, and Callie bit her lip. She'd been about to ask Braden if that was okay. She wasn't going to get into that habit again. So far, she and Braden had a good relationship, an equal partnership. Greg had been the domineering one in her past relationship, and she wasn't going down that path again. She didn't need to ask permission for decisions she made.

'Is she okay?' Braden finally asked.

'Her pains are really close and we've been waiting for the doctor. There's been a car accident and they're waiting for an ambulance.'

'That's not good. I was worried the siren was for Fallon. Callie?'

'Yes,' she said slowly, picking up the hesitation in his voice. 'What's wrong?'

'Is Laura there?'

'Not yet, but apparently there's a staff shortage and she's on her way. I'm waiting out the front to take her in.'

'I'm sorry I snapped at you at the pub, love. But Laura said something really strange and I'm worried about why she's here. I'm really sorry. It's no excuse but I took it out on you when I saw you being friendly to her.'

'What did she say?'

'I'll tell you later, but in the meantime, she's got me worried. I think she's here to cause trouble.'

'Okay,' Callie said slowly. 'I didn't get that impression. She was quite friendly to me.'

'I don't trust her.'

'Why?'

'Just be careful what you say, Callie.'

'What's that supposed to mean?' She lowered her voice. 'She's coming now. I'll have to go.'

'Okay, I'll sleep on the sofa here. Let me know when the baby's born. I hope everything goes well, and Callie?'

'Yes?' she said as Laura walked up the steps towards her.

'I love you. I'm sorry for being a brute.'

She hesitated and the call disconnected. Callie turned to meet Laura, wondering what the newcomer had said to upset Braden so much.

How could she possibly be a threat to them?

# Chapter 10

*Laura*

As Laura drove the four blocks from the hotel to the hospital, she wondered why the hell she'd offered to help. The offer had sprung to her lips naturally, as it would have a few years ago when she was still working in midwifery. And she hadn't given any thought to how she'd feel. Or how she'd felt for the last three years

Oh, she had no doubt she could deliver the baby and deal with any emergency that might come up, but it was her emotional well-being that she'd ignored. When she'd first left work, she couldn't even cope with seeing a pregnant woman or a mother with a young baby without going to pieces.

It had lasted so long Brett had finally lost patience with her.

*Forget about it. Forget about him.*

As Laura locked the hire car and put the keys in her bag her hands began to sweat, despite the cool of the evening.

Callie was waiting for her at the main entrance and Laura walked towards the steps. She forced herself into the present. There was a staff shortage here, she'd offered to help, and she would do so without making a fool of herself. She would try anyway; it was time to stop being selfish and wallowing in her own self-pity. Tonight, there was a woman, a harried doctor and a short-staffed maternity ward in need, so she'd do her absolute best.

A loud scream came from inside as she walked up the steps.

Callie's eyes widened. 'That was Fallon,' she said, taking off into the hospital. Laura hurried after her.

'She's just down here,' Callie said. 'The third door on the right.'

'Is Dr Harry with her?'

'No, he's been in Emergency. There's only Jon and her mum and me. None of us has any idea what to do.'

'How close are her pains?' Laura asked.

'Pretty close, I guess. Only a couple of minutes apart.'

Laura nodded and looked around as they hurried down the corridor. She spotted what she was looking for on the left. 'You go and tell her I'm on my way. I'll be there as soon as I find a gown and get scrubbed up.'

Callie nodded and went into the room across the corridor.

Laura quickly found a long-sleeved green disposable gown, and a sink to wash her hands. Crossing to the cupboard, she found an instrument pack for the delivery. She picked up a box of gloves and wheeled out the portable patient monitor that was in the room. Having to focus in a new environment helped clear her head. The excitement of the imminent delivery of a new baby took over, and she calmed.

*You've got this,* she thought.

As Laura entered the labour ward Fallon was standing beside the bed, her hands gripping the rails as she bent over, dragging in deep breaths. Laura quickly looked around, satisfied to see that the rest of the equipment was in the room.

'Looks like that baby's ready to arrive,' Laura said briskly. 'Jon, can you help Fallon onto the bed so I can take a look, and we'll know more about what's happening?' She smiled at the older woman sitting in the soft sofa chair looking worried. 'Hello, I'm Laura, the midwife, and we'll look after Fallon. Your daughter?'

The woman nodded. 'Thank you, Laura. I'm Ruth.'

'I'm just going to examine your daughter.'

'How about we grab a coffee, Ruth?' Callie took Ruth's arm. 'I saw a coffee machine in the waiting room. I think we could all do with one. What about you, Jon?'

Her husband was standing beside the bed, and Laura waited until he nodded and reached over and kissed Fallon's cheek. 'I won't be far away,' he said.

'Thank you, Callie,' Laura said.

Fallon was soon lying on the bed, between contractions, and Laura pulled the curtain around to give her privacy. It didn't take very long to discover that the baby was indeed ready to be born. Fallon's blood pressure was fine and the baby's heartbeat was strong.

'That's why you've been in so much intense pain, Fallon. You've fully dilated already and this bub is ready to come and meet you. Now, who would you like here with you for the birth? It's not going to take very long now.'

Footsteps sounded in the corridor, and there was a tap on the door.

Laura pulled the gloves off and checked that Fallon was comfortable before she pulled the curtain open.

Dr Higgins was standing just inside the door. 'Thank you, Laura. I'm sorry I wasn't here. It's been a very busy evening. There's been a serious car accident out on the highway and I've just sent one patient to Charleville. I've admitted his wife, she has a broken arm and I suspect a slight concussion. She's in X-ray now.'

'That's not good,' Laura said. 'Have you got someone to help you down there?'

'One nurse, thank goodness. And the X-ray technician was in town for the weekend; Larissa goes out with one of the paramedics and he lives in town. They'd just arrived from Charleville when I called.'

'It seems like a very short-staffed establishment.'

'The rest of the staff have gone down with that vomiting bug this weekend, but we do depend on a lot of locum staff. Specialists and the like fly in from the city and stay here for a week or two at a time. We have trouble getting permanent qualified staff.'

'Have you been here long?'

Harry raised his eyebrows as she asked. 'Just under a month. You don't know how much I appreciate you being here tonight.'

A slight moan came from the bed and the doctor turned to the patient. 'I'm sorry, Mrs Ingram. You've got more things to think about than the issues down in Emergency. I apologise I should've stepped outside with Laura and left you in peace.' He moved closer to the bed and smiled at her. 'So how are you feeling?'

'Nervous,' she said. 'But keen to get this over and done with.'

'Trust me, this will be one of the most beautiful experiences of your life.' His voice was soft and seemed to calm Fallon. 'There's nothing like seeing a mum give birth for the first time.'

Laura moved closer to them. 'Everything is going very well, Dr Higgins. Perfect blood pressure, the baby's heartbeat is nice and strong and Mrs Ingram—'

Fallon shook her head. 'Fallon, please. Not Mrs Ingram.'

Laura smiled and continued. 'And Fallon is fully dilated and ready to deliver.'

'Any medication?' Harry asked.

Laura shook her head. 'Not from here.'

'So, who would you like in here for the birth, Fallon?' Dr Harry asked.

Fallon glanced across to Laura. 'I was going to have my mum but I don't know that she's up to it.'

'Would you like me to go and ask her?' Laura said.

'Please, and if Mum says no, see if Callie will come in. And Jon, of course. He has to be here to see our baby born.'

Fallon put her head back and moaned. 'Oh God, give me an auto-rotating helicopter any day. At least I know what to do there.'

Laura frowned and then twigged. 'You're a helicopter pilot?'

'I was.' Fallon began to pant. 'And I will be again.' She squeezed her face up in a grimace as another contraction built.

'I'll go down to the waiting room and get them,' Harry said. 'Laura, you prepare Fallon and we'll get this show on the road.'

He winked at Fallon as he headed to the door.

# Chapter 11

*Callie*

Ryan James Ingram weighed in at a healthy three and a half kilograms, and the birth had been one of the most incredible experiences of Callie's life. She had no idea the emotion that Jon and Fallon would be feeling if she was feeling this way.

The birth had been quick and relatively easy. Ryan had been born only ten minutes after Callie had gone back into the ward.

When Harry had come to get them, Ruth had been shaking and decided she wasn't up to going in for the birth. 'I don't want Fallon to have to worry about me and I know she will. I honestly don't think I can stand to be in there and see her in so much pain. I don't want her to see me worried. I'll just sit out here in the waiting room and wait. She should be with Jon.' Ruth couldn't seem to stop talking. 'And Callie, I know she wants you in there. Are you happy to be there?'

Callie had looked at Harry and Harry nodded.

'Yes, she said she wanted me for support and I'll be okay.'

Being present at the birth of Ryan James Ingram had been a life-changing moment for Callie. She had been privileged to see the look of love on Jon's face as he'd lifted his son and then placed the newborn on Fallon's stomach.

Fallon's face was wreathed in a huge smile as Laura took over. Jon walked around the side of the bed to where Callie had supported Fallon's shoulders during the delivery. When he put his cheek against Fallon's, the expression on his face and the sight of him brushing a tear away almost brought Callie undone.

'We have a beautiful little boy, sweetheart,' he said.

'I'll leave you two to have time together and I'll go and tell Ruth she's got a grandson,' Callie whispered quietly

Fallon reached up and squeezed her hand. 'Thank you, Cal. I'll never forget you being here with me tonight.'

Dr Harry chuckled. 'See, I told you, you'd soon forget the pain, Fallon.'

'It wasn't anywhere near as bad as I was expecting,' Fallon said. 'And I had no pain relief.'

'A natural birth,' Laura said with a smile. 'You did well.'

Callie's throat clogged with emotion. She swallowed and took a deep breath. It was hard to leave. She nodded at Dr Harry. 'Thank you for letting me be here.'

As she turned to leave, she was taken aback to see Laura standing at the end of the bed. She'd swaddled the baby and handed him over to Fallon. Fallon was nursing him. Laura stood there staring at them and tears ran down her cheeks.

Callie was surprised. It was such a difference from the brisk, businesslike midwife who had taken Fallon through the birth.

Laura was staring at her hands, white from being gripped tightly in front of her. She lifted her head and looked at Fallon holding her newborn. Her eyes were full of pain and her mouth was twisted in a tight grimace as she fought tears. This wasn't joy in the birth; this was some sort of deep hurt. Callie's heart went out to her, and she wasn't sure what to do.

Dr Harry was with Fallon and Jon, looking at the baby when Laura realised Callie was looking at her.

She straightened and pulled a handkerchief from her pocket and wiped her eyes. The smile she directed at Callie was tremulous. 'A beautiful experience.' She turned to Dr Harry. 'Thank you for letting me assist, Dr Higgins.'

Harry walked across to Laura and took her hand. 'Thank you very much for helping us out, Laura. I can't interest you in a job at the hospital, can I?'

As Callie walked out the door, she wondered what Laura's answer would be.

# Chapter 12

*Callie*

Ten minutes later Callie walked slowly down the steps of the hospital. It was dark outside and a security light flashed on as she walked down the steps. Ruth had wanted to drive her home, but Callie had insisted on walking.

'It's a beautiful night and not far to go and I don't want to rush you. I think Braden wants to go home so we won't wait unless he's decided to stay.'

Ruth gave her a hug and the last she saw of Ruth was her running down the corridor to the labour ward.

The way Callie was feeling, she needed some time alone, and the walk down to the Malone house would give her some time to process her thoughts.

The night was quiet and the sky crystal clear. Callie looked up at the stars, her feelings chaotic. Euphoria mixed with sadness; her emotions so pumped she didn't even feel the cold through her light cardigan and summer jeans. When she reached the corner opposite the Catholic church, she stopped walking and took a deep breath.

Watching Ryan making his way into the world, and supporting Fallon had been wonderful, but the experience also made her sad. She couldn't stop thinking about Julia and the three little boys she had given birth to. Three little boys she would never see grow up. Tears filled her eyes as she crossed the road. How did Braden cope with that knowledge every day? How hard must it have been for him to not only lose his wife but to lose the mother of his boys? Callie had thought she'd had sympathy for his circumstance before, but now, a gut-wrenching sadness consumed her

As she walked along Annie Street, she pondered the experience that she'd been a part of. The birth had made her think about something that she'd not given much thought to until Braden had mentioned it.

Did she want to have children? Did Braden really want more children, as he'd said? More children with her?

Was she prepared to risk leaving a child motherless? Who knew what life would bring in the future? Nothing was certain.

Callie knew she had to think about where their relationship was going. She loved Braden and the boys, and she had settled right into the community but was beginning to doubt whether becoming a true family unit was the right thing. A family she knew Braden wanted to grow even more.

She and Braden hadn't had much of a chance to talk about what had happened since Nigel's appointment with the child psychologist; in fact, Braden had shut down a little since that day and she wondered what was going on in his head.

The way he'd snapped at her in the pub tonight had hurt, when all she'd done was show Laura friendship. How well did she know Braden? Now that the first flush of romance and the initial excitement of their engagement was over, the doubt pressed in.

Had she made a huge mistake? Should she leave Augathella? Tears misted her eyes again. The thought of leaving Braden and the boys was heartbreaking.

But it seemed as though the honeymoon period was over and they were now living what real life was.

Callie pulled a face. *The honeymoon's over and I haven't even had the wedding.*

Her fingers played with the engagement ring on her left hand and she tried to stay positive as she approached the house.

Was marrying Braden the right thing to do? Or had Braden just thought that he'd fallen in love with her because he was lonely and he needed a mother for the boys?

Callie had no doubt she loved Braden and she *did* want to spend the rest of her life with him and the boys, but what she wanted and what was the right thing to do were two different things.

And the only way to come to that decision was to sit down with Brayden and have an honest, boots and all talk. Then she could make a decision and rest easy, knowing she had considered what was right.

As she approached the Malone house, a single light was burning on the front porch, and the rest of the house was in darkness. Their—no, Braden's—wagon was parked on the footpath.

Tonight wasn't the right time to discuss her doubts. Too many things had happened that had left her feeling uncertain.

Laura, the unexpected visitor, had upset Braden.

It had been a happy night for Fallon and Jon, and Callie didn't want the memory of this special night to be flawed by a difficult talk with Brayden. Because she knew it was going to be hard, and he wouldn't appreciate what she was thinking. Maybe she was totally off base, but she'd worried ever since Nigel had let his feelings be known. And that showed her that she suspected what the outcome would be.

It also wasn't right to have such a discussion in someone else's home or in the car driving back to Kilcoy Station

Callie decided to bide her time and see what happened over the next few days.

# Chapter 13

*Braden*

Braden woke with a start when he heard a door open and close quietly. He didn't remember stretching out on the lounge, but he and Nigel were now lengthways on the soft sofa. Nigel was tucked into his side, his little chest rising and falling evenly as he slept. Braden eased himself away carefully, but Nigel didn't stir. He made sure Nigel was comfortable and dropped a kiss on his forehead before he stood and stretched.

Before he could walk into the hall and see who was at the door, Callie appeared in the doorway.

He smiled and held his arms open. As she came over to him her smile was shaky, and her eyes filled with tears. She stepped into his arms and he held her tight.

'What's wrong, love? Did something happen? Is Fallon all right?'

Callie shook her head and he felt the sob escape from her as he rested his head on top of hers. Dread pooled in his stomach

'The baby?' he asked quietly.

Callie took a deep breath and looked up at him. He used his thumb to gently wipe away the tears hovering on her bottom eyelids.

'Fallon is fine. Ryan James Ingram weighed in at three and a half kilos. He's a bonny little bub, and they are ecstatic.'

'And he's fine? Fallon's okay?'

'Yes, and so's Jon.' Callie nodded. 'Ryan has two arms, two legs, ten fingers and toes, a head of blond fuzz and a lusty cry. He's beautiful, Braden.' Her voice trembled again.

'So, what's wrong, love? Have I upset you?'

She shook her head. 'I'm just emotional. It was a pretty amazing experience. I was honoured to be there.'

He pulled her close again. 'That it is.'

They stood quietly for a few moments until Callie pulled back and gestured to Nigel. 'Are the boys okay? Was Nigel upset again?'

'He woke up and I've been snoozing with him on the sofa.'

Braden was relieved when Callie reached up and cupped his cheek. 'You look tired.'

'I am a bit. I had a big day, and I'm disappointed that we didn't get our night together.' Callie stepped back and he sensed her withdrawal.

'But I'm pleased that the baby's arrived and that it all went well.' He tried to keep his voice casual. 'Did Laura end up helping Harry?'

'She did, and she was marvellous.' Callie frowned. 'But I was worried about her at the end. She looked really upset and she was crying when I left. She was really efficient and kind during the birth though. Why did she upset you so much? I thought she seemed nice. What did she say to you?'

'She accused me of womanising, drinking and being a lousy father to start with. You came in for a serve too. My new wife, she'd heard apparently.'

Callie's mouth dropped open in shock. 'What? Where on earth would she have heard that? Is that why she's here?'

'She believes that she has responsibility for the boys. The boys who are *being neglected*. She's come to see whether I'm a suitable father or not.'

'That's ridiculous.'

'I've been thinking about it a bit. She has a point. I did abandon them. Depends what she's heard.'

Callie clutched his arm. 'For goodness' sake, you'd just lost your wife. And they weren't abandoned, they were with Sophie. And where on earth would she have heard that? She's come from New Zealand!'

'Maybe. I still carry responsibility for the way Nigel is though. He's not a happy little boy.'

'And you're seeking professional help for him. They have a wonderful home and a wonderful father. They're all happy at school, and you'll get through this difficult time with Nigel.'

'*I* will?' He looked at her curiously. '*We* will.'

Cold touched his heart when she looked away, but he didn't press the issue. Braden knew Callie had seen his angry side when he'd snapped at her about inviting Laura to stay. He wished he could take those words back.

'What do you want to do?' he asked.

Her head flew up. 'Do?'

'Will we stay here for the night or go home?'

'I don't mind. What do you want to do?'

'I guess we're here now and the boys are settled. Ruth wanted to make up a bed for us in the spare bedroom. If we stay in town, we can visit Fallon tomorrow, and then go home.'

Callie lifted her eyes to meet his. 'And sort out Laura? I'm sorry I made it difficult for you.'

'No, I should have kept my temper, but Callie, she terrified me. How could she come here and say things like that? I don't want her out at the station, but she is entitled to meet the boys.'

'Maybe if she did stay out there, she'd see what a good home they have?'

Braden shook his head. 'I don't know. I don't know what to think.'

'I think,' Callie said slowly, 'she is a troubled lady. Do you know anything about her? Is she married? Does she have kids?'

'She's married. I know that because we couldn't go to the wedding because Julia was just about to have Rory, and the wedding was in the Cotswolds where they grew up. She'd been to New Zealand on a holiday and met a guy, but they were to get married in the UK. I saw photos, but to be honest, Julia and Laura were never close.'

Callie went to speak, but before she could the back door opened.

'Here's Ruth now. Are you happy to stay?' he asked quickly.

Callie nodded. 'Yes. You stay here with Nigel and I'll sleep in with the boys.'

Braden wasn't happy with that arrangement but could see the wisdom of it. It made no more work for Ruth. 'Good idea.'

Ruth was in the kitchen and they heard the tap turn on and the kettle fill. 'Ah, the inevitable cup of tea,' Braden said with a smile. 'Come on, I'll go congratulate the new grandmother.'

He was pleased when Callie slipped her hand into his. They walked into the living room together.

When Ruth burst into tears, Braden let go of Callie and hugged her.

'I'm a granny,' Ruth said, with a huge smile through her happy tears.

# Chapter 14

*Laura*

Laura walked up the stairs to the first floor of the Augathella Hotel. The carpet had a slightly mouldy smell, and she didn't hold out much hope for the room. She'd retrieved her suitcase from the car when she'd moved it to the car park at the back of the hotel. Heading up the stairs she looked for room four and when she found it, she slid the key into the lock. To her surprise, the room was freshly-painted and nicely decorated. Two white rolled towels and a sprig of native flowers sat on a pale blue candlewick bedspread, with soft-looking dark blue European pillows at the head of the bed.

She turned to the bathroom and again was pleasantly surprised by a recently renovated bathroom, fitted out in modern colours with a huge inviting bathtub along one wall. Without thinking, Laura kicked off her shoes, tuned the taps on and opened one of the sachets of bath salts that sat in a glass jar at the edge of the bath. Catching a glimpse of her face in the mirror, she held back a groan. Her eyes were red-rimmed and purple shadows filled the gaunt hollows beneath them.

She went back out to the bedroom and lifted her suitcase onto the luggage rack, before opening the mini-bar refrigerator. A selection of small bottles of wine and spirits, and assorted soft drinks and bottled water met her gaze. She picked out a small bottle of white wine, found a glass on the counter top and headed to the bathroom.

After a day like she'd had, she deserved some luxury. Slipping off her suit and draping it carefully over the towel rack, she eased herself into the warm bubbled water and put the glass of wine on the timber caddy across the middle of the bathtub.

Whoever would have thought she would find this in the middle of the outback? It was as good—if not better— as the hotel she'd stayed at in Brisbane when she'd landed from Auckland the day before yesterday.

Was it only two days ago? The events of the past twelve hours made it feel like a week or more.

She'd met her brother-in-law and his partner, and their friends. She'd met a very handsome doctor and delivered a baby.

A doctor who'd offered her a job.

And to Laura's utter shock, she realised that she was considering it. What better way to see what Braden was really doing, and how the three little boys were? Settle into the town for a while, get to know people and she would see what was really happening.

Sipping the chilled wine, she put her head back and closed her eyes as the warmth enveloped her. Despite the long trip, the hard day that had culminated in her confronting her demons, Laura began to relax.

Maybe coming to the back of nowhere to check on her nephews had been a good move. This was the best she'd felt for a long time. Shedding tears after that sweet little bub had been born seemed to have shifted something inside her.

Before she got her hopes up that things had finally changed for her, she would wait.

Tomorrow was another day.

\*\*\*

Harry was pleased that the pub was shut when he left the hospital a bit after ten. The thought of another glass of whisky was way too tempting. It had been a very different day from what he'd anticipated when he'd set off for the hospital with his novel under his arm that morning.

He hadn't expected to be invited to join the locals for dinner, he hadn't expected to finish the day in the labour ward, or to deal with a car accident, and he certainly hadn't expected to meet a woman he now couldn't get out of his thoughts.

The look of vulnerability on Laura Adnum's face when he had first seen her at the door of the pub tonight was the one that stayed uppermost in his mind.

She was a beautiful woman, the personification of elegance. The way she held herself, the way she dressed, and her cultured voice combined to create a mysterious woman.

He was curious why she was in Augathella; Laura looked more suited to a high tea at the Ritz. He'd enjoyed talking to her over dinner, and he'd been impressed by her professionalism in the delivery room later in the night.

When he'd offered her a job she'd shown a spark of interest, and he'd been pleased when she'd waited at the hospital until he was ready to leave, giving him the perfect opportunity for them to talk. They'd chatted for over half an hour and Harry knew in that short time he wanted to spend more time with her. That knowledge alone had shocked him, and he'd waited for Jenny's voice to bring him to his senses, but his mind had been silent.

He'd taken her hand as they'd said goodnight. 'Laura?'

Her eyes met his. 'Yes, Harry?'

'I was wondering whether you'd like to keep me company tomorrow. Unless you have other plans of course. I have to drive north to the next town to visit a patient.'

'A home visit?' she asked with a smile. 'That's unusual these days.'

'It is.'

He waited for her reply and felt like jumping with a fist pump when she did.

'What time and where shall I meet you?'

# Chapter 15

*Callie*

Braden and Callie skirted around each other in Ruth's kitchen the following morning. They were all up early; the boys had been up and out to feed the chooks at six-thirty. Ruth was already baking when Callie followed them to make sure they were quiet.

'What on earth are you doing at this time of the morning, Ruth?'

Mixing bowls lined the bench, and portions of flour, sugar and butter were sitting along the benchtop.

'I didn't want to start the Mixmaster until you were all awake.'

Callie looked up as Braden appeared in the doorway from the living room, hair tousled and unshaven. Her heart skipped a beat, and she ignored it. She'd had little sleep; the bed was very hard, her thoughts had gone round and round, and the overpowering smell of mothballs had been hard to ignore.

'Why are you baking? I thought you were all packed up to move. Isn't the house settling next week?'

Ben Riley had bought the house from Fallon's Great Uncle George, now a resident of the aged care facility at the back of the hospital. Ben and his partner, Amelia and her dog, Chilli Girl were moving in the weekend after next.

'We are, but I promised to help Jenny Riley with the catering for her RFDS garden party. It's next Saturday. If I'd known that Fallon was going to have little Ryan a month early, I never would have promised.' Ruth reached a hand up to smooth her hair back and left a streak of flour on her forehead.

'How much do you have to bake?' Callie asked, keeping her eyes on Braden as he walked over to the kettle and helped himself to the jar of instant coffee. She hid a smile; one thing she'd learned about Braden over the past months, was that he wasn't a morning person, and there was no point trying to talk to him before he'd had his first coffee.

'Six sponge cakes and four dozen lamingtons. And then I said I'd help with the sandwiches on Saturday morning, but now I'll be out of town at Fallon and Jon's place. I can't cook there because they have a combustion stove and I don't know it well enough, plus I'll be busy helping with the baby. I feel bad letting Jenny down, so I thought I'd get the cakes made for the lamingtons today and freeze them, ready to roll in the chocolate and coconut the afternoon before. I can do that without an oven.'

'I'm sure Jenny will understand, and I'm sure we can find someone else to step in,' Callie said. 'At worst, I can do some baking next Thursday. I'm not working at the school that day.'

'Oh really? That would be a great help. I know I'm going to be busy with Fallon, because she'll need me to buy some more things for the baby. We were planning to go down to Charleville this week and get the last few things for the baby's room. We never thought there'd be a baby in there before we were finished.'

'How long will they stay in hospital?' Callie asked.

'Dr Harry said at least three days so I can go down to Charleville tomorrow with a shopping list, and then Jon and I can get everything ready before they go home.'

Callie turned to Braden and made a judgment call when she saw the glass mug was half-empty. 'What time did you want to head home this morning? Is there anything you have to do in town?'

Braden put the cup down and nodded. 'I would like to catch up with Laura before we leave.'

Braden and Callie exchanged a look. She knew it would be to sort out whether Laura was going to come out and stay with them at the station.

'It's a bit early to go to see her at the hotel now,' Callie said. 'So, you keep the boys entertained for a while and I'll give Ruth a hand here.'

She waved away Ruth's objections. 'No arguments, Ruth. You have a busy week ahead. If we'd known that we wouldn't have foisted the boys on you last night.'

'They were fine. I love having them here.' Ruth was almost bursting with excitement. 'And now we have our own little boy to look forward to spoiling.'

'Well, you sure spoil these three,' Braden chipped in.

The boys under discussion were sitting at the table having toast and vegemite fingers.

'Dad, I want to come too. Where are you going? Don't leave me here by myself,' Nigel said loudly.

'You won't be by yourself, mate.' Braden drained the last of his coffee. 'Callie's here and Rory and Petie will be too. Ruth's going to do lots of baking and I'm sure there'll be bowls and beaters to lick.'

Ruth nodded. 'There will. I'll need help cleaning them.'

'I don't want to lick the bowls today. I want to come with you. Where are you going, Dad?'

Braden sighed; he knew he'd gone easy on Nigel lately, but his middle son had to learn that he couldn't call the shots. But Braden was very aware of what the child psychologist had said.

'Give him a little bit of leeway for a few weeks.'

'I have to go into town and see somebody and if you stay here, I'll bring you a surprise. All of you.'

'No, I want to come with you now. Who are you going to see? Someone I know too?'

'No mate, it's a stranger.'

'We shouldn't talk to strangers,' Petie piped up.

'That's right,' Nigel agreed. 'Why are you talking to a stranger? I'll come and look after you, Dad.'

Braden caught Callie's eye over the top of Nigel's head. She grinned and nodded.

'Okay, mate, you can come with me, but you have to promise me that you're going to bring your good manners with you and be on your best behaviour.'

'Yay, I'm going with Dad. I'm going with Dad and you're not,' Nigel yelled in a sing-song voice and poked Rory with his elbow.

'I don't care. I want to stay here and lick the bowls,' Rory said calmly. He'd been so good with

97

Nigel's tantrums that Braden called his eldest son his little peacekeeper.

Nigel jumped up and headed for the door, barely warranting a glance from Petie and Rory.

Braden and Callie followed him outside.

'Do you want me to come with you? Are you okay with talking to her?'

Even though Nigel was with them Braden reached out and put his arms around Callie.

'I'll be fine. I'll be patient and stay calm. I'm just going to go and see Laura and see how long she intends staying. Then I can organise for her to meet the boys. She's entitled to. She can meet this little scallywag today and then we'll take it from there.'

'Will you ask her to stay at the property?'

'I'll see,' he said. 'I'll see what her plans are.' Braden grinned. 'Who knows, she might decide to move here. She might fall in love with Augathella like someone else I know.'

'Don't joke about it,' Callie said. She stood on her tiptoes and brushed her lips across his. 'And there was a huge attraction in Augathella for me.'

'That was nice, 'Braden murmured.

'Ergh,' Nigel said. 'I'm never going to kiss girls.'

Callie grabbed him and kissed his cheek. 'I'm not a girl so I can kiss your cheek. I'm a grown-up.' She ruffled his hair. 'You be a good boy for Dad, won't you, and when you get back, I'm sure Ruth will have some cake for us to take home.'

Braden opened the door and Nigel jumped in the front seat; his grin was filled with pride. 'Callie, you tell Petie and Rory that I got to ride in the front,' he said.

'I'm sure they'll be extremely jealous,' Callie agreed, as she frowned at Braden.

'We're only going around the corner, Cal,' he said. 'I'll park up the road.'

\*\*\*

Braden blew Callie another kiss and started the car. She was so good for him. He was a very lucky man. A calm feeling descended on him as he drove into town, Nigel chatting happily beside him. It was only a matter of minutes before he pulled up outside the pub.

Laura had told him as she left to go to the hospital last night that she would get her own room because she didn't feel right taking theirs.

Braden had shrugged and said, 'Whatever.'

At that stage, the anger had still been with him after what Laura had said about him being a lousy father.

There was only one car parked at the back of the pub and he assumed it was hers. He raised his eyebrows.

*A silver Jaguar sedan.*

She certainly wasn't short of a quid if that was her car. He wouldn't want to see it heading out to Kilcoy Station on the dirt road.

That thought brought a smile to his face as he remembered the day he'd met Callie. She had driven out there in her low-slung red sports car. Their meeting had taken place as he had retrieved her expensive luggage when it had almost been swept away in the irrigation channel.

Callie's red sports car still sat in the shed at the station and he often offered to go for a drive with her.

'Nope. It'll get dirty again. I'm going to sell it soon.'

'What are you waiting for?' he'd asked.

Her reply had worried him.

'I'm not ready yet. That's part of my old life, that's the old Callie.' But her grin was wide and Braden decided he was being super sensitive.

'The new Callie drives a four-wheel drive on dirt roads,' she added. 'A ute that takes little dogs on the tray back, has kids in the back, plus crates of schoolwork *and* leaves *plenty* of room for cakes.'

'I liked the old Callie, but I like the new one too,' he'd said.

*He loved the new Callie.*

Braden was very much looking forward to the day when Callie became Mrs Cartwright. His ring was on her finger, and she'd agreed to marry him, but now she wanted to wait until Nigel was sorted. He knew Callie wasn't happy at the moment and that his temper last night had again set off her doubts that had surfaced when Nigel had had his hissy fit a few weeks back.

He glanced across at his middle son as he parked the car, and decided to take advantage of having Nigel in the car with him.

'Can we have a chat, Nige?'

'Yep, what about?' Nigel's voice was wary. 'And before you get cross, I did do my homework the other day. I really did lose it.'

'I didn't know about your missing homework.'

'Oops,' Nigel said, but he giggled. 'Tweedle chewed it.'

Braden pulled a disbelieving face. 'The dog ate your homework, hey? Nuh, doesn't cut it, mate. You have to be more imaginative than that.'

'He really did, Dad. The slobber was awesome, but it really grossed Miss Mason right out.'

'Poor Miss Mason. I'm glad she's your teacher. She's a nice lady. So was that lady doctor down in Charleville. What did you think about talking to her?'

Braden saw the moment that Nigel began to shut down and he regretted saying anything.

'It's okay. I just want to know if you like her. And if you want to keep going there.'

'She's okay. I like the toys she's got in her office.'

'Okay, that's all I needed to know.'

There was silence for a while and Nigel picked at a blister on his thumb.

'Daddy?'

Braden looked across at him; it was unusual for Nigel to call him Daddy; he'd been Dad for a year or so now.

'Yes, mate.'

'What if I said I don't want to talk to her again? Would you be cranky?'

'Of course not. You don't have to go if you don't want to, but maybe you could tell me why you don't.'

'She talks about stupid things like Miss Shaw does at school.

Brayden thought carefully. Miss Shaw was the school counsellor; he wasn't aware that she was talking to Nigel.

'Sometimes, mate, it helps to talk to people about things that we're worried about. I knew you were worried about something when you got upset that day and I thought that talking to someone might help you.'

'I'd rather talk to you and Callie,' he said quietly. 'And yeah, I probably should say sorry to Callie cause some of those words I said to her were pretty mean.'

Braden couldn't help the grin on his face. 'I think that would make Callie very, very happy. I know it would make me very happy.'

'She still loves me though, because she kissed me just now.'

'She does love you, mate. She loves all of us, we are very lucky men.'

Nigel nodded and reached for the door handle. 'Okay, Dad, that's enough of the sooky talk. And I really don't mind if you kiss Callie. I think that's what dads and mums do.'

Braden took a breath. 'Mums?' he said.

'Callie is going to be our new mum, isn't she?'

'Callie won't be your new mum until she's sure that that's the best thing for you and Petie and Rory.'

Nigel's face was a picture. He screwed up his little snub nose and shook his head. His freckles stood out on his fair skin. A surge of love went through Braden and he reached over and put his arm around him. 'Come here, mate. Give your dad a hug.'

That was enough talking, Braden decided. He wouldn't push the issue of Callie being their new mum but the conversation he'd had with Nigel had been encouraging.

'I'll only say one more thing, Nige. If you want to talk to Callie, you go ahead and talk to her.'

'Okay, Dad. Now, who are we going to see? A stranger?'

Braden wondered whether it was the right time to go and see Laura so soon after having their conversation. He didn't want to undo all the good that had been gained by this little chat.

'Just someone who's come to visit our town. You can call her Aunty Laura if you want.'

'Okay, and then can we go to the rural store?'

'You sure are a little cowboy, aren't you, mate? What do you want at the rural store?'

'I want a new rope for some tricks with Tweedle.'

Braden relaxed as their talking got into much easier territory. 'I guess we can go to the store afterwards. Damn, no we can't. It's Sunday. I don't think it's open.'

'It is, Dad. It's open from nine till twelve on Sundays.'

Braden shook his head. 'How do you know that?'

'We talked about it in class at school, when we were learning the big clock. The real one with the hands.'

'Okay, you've won me. We'll go to the store as soon as we visit Laura. I mean Aunty Laura.' It still stuck in Braden's throat to say that. 'Then we've got to go and get Callie and your brothers and head home. I've got a lot of work to do this afternoon.'

'And I can't wait to see Tweedle,' Nigel said, his face screwed unhappily in a frown.

'What's wrong now?' Braden was getting tired. It was easier to round up a bunch of steers than spend half an hour in the car with Nigel.

'Did you know that Amelia's moving into Aunty Ruth's house?'

'I did.'

'And she's taking Chilli Girl with her.'

'Is that a problem? Does it bother you?'

'No, but I want to know whether our dogs can go and visit Chilli Girl. They'll be okay because they have friends at our station, but Chilli is going to be very lonely.'

'That's very thoughtful of you. I'm sure we can organise something because Amelia will still be working out at our station. Come on, we'll go and meet Aunty Laura or we'll never get home.'

'Never? Really and truly, we'd never get home again? Where would we go instead? Where would we live?' Nigel's eyes were wide. 'What about the dogs?'

Braden chuckled. 'Just an expression, mate. Come on, follow me.'

# Chapter 16

*Laura*

Laura was dressed and almost ready before Harry arrived to take her out for the day. She'd thought long and hard about what she was going to wear; she didn't want to look as though she'd gone to too much trouble, but she didn't want to look too casual. Harry had said they'd go out for lunch in Tambo, but she hadn't asked where.

A pub? A flash restaurant? A country house? All required a different style of dress, and one thing that was very important to Laura was fitting in. Her dress sense helped her with that. If she was nicely dressed and made up, she could blend into any setting. People tended to look at her exterior appearance and didn't look too closely and realise that she was usually a bundle of nerves inside.

And she had no idea what sort of town Tambo was, and she didn't have time to Google it before she got dressed. On the way out to Augathella, she'd come through some different-sized towns, but they'd all looked fairly casual, so she'd decided not to dress up too much today. She'd been way overdressed for the pub dinner last night. In the end, she settled for a pair of good jeans, a short-sleeved white T-shirt and a pretty shirt that tied in a knot at her waist. she slipped on a pair of running shoes and put a pair of sandals into her large bag just in case it was a dressy establishment.

There was a tap on the door and her eyes widened in surprise. Harry was early and she was supposed to meet him downstairs. She didn't feel comfortable about him coming up to her room. Had she made another mistake by trusting a man?

'Just a moment, please.' She reached for her bag and quickly checked her hair in the mirror above the bench.

'Laura. it's Braden. I'll go and wait downstairs if you've got time for a chat. Does that suit?'

'Thank you, Braden. Yes, I would very much like to have a chat with you. I'm going out shortly, so it'll have to be quick.'

Laura was very surprised that Braden Cartwright was outside her door. She had really thought she wouldn't see him again until she drove back out to the cattle station. The impression of him last night had not been one bit favourable and had matched all that she'd been told.

But his voice this morning—albeit through a closed door—had sounded quite civil.

Laura tucked the strap of her large red leather bag over her shoulder and picked up her light coat. Even though it was much warmer out here than she'd expected, there was a chance that the wind could turn cool.

She regretted that she hadn't researched her trip more thoroughly. A knee-jerk reaction after the house sale had settled had seen her buying a plane ticket and taking the first available flight out of New Zealand to Brisbane, and then hiring a car and driving west.

The trip had been a shock. Used to soft green hilly landscapes, the red dust and scraggy trees lining the flat roads had surprised Laura. For the first few hundred kilometres, it had been a novelty and she'd waited for the landscape to change, but it hadn't. Flat roads edged with yellow paddocks had changed into flat landscapes and red dirt. She'd known nothing about the towns she passed through and then arrived at, and she knew even less about Braden and his boys. She had heard nothing from him since Julia had been killed.

Foolishly Laura had set off for a great unknown. She now wondered why she had done so, and what was ahead of her.

Locking the door behind her, she put the key in her bag and headed for the stairs. She had decided to book the room for three nights until she'd found out what she wanted to know.

Biting her lip, she thought about it. She guessed she needed to know that her sister's boys were safe and well cared for.

But she had her doubts.

The Augathella pub—one of two in town, she'd been told by Reg last night—was a beautiful old building. Diamond-shaped stained-glass windows let in light from outside over the timber staircase with an ornately carved banister. A crystal chandelier hung from the ceiling. The building was gorgeous and with a bit of decorating downstairs could be even better. She'd had no idea of the age of the building until she'd gone up the staircase to the second floor last night.

Braden was waiting just inside the door downstairs.

'Good morning, Laura. I hope you don't mind me just calling in. I asked Mark, the pub manager, which room you were in, and he suggested I go up and knock to let you know I was here. There aren't any phones in the rooms, or he would have called you. I hope that was okay.'

'Yes, that's fine.' Laura kept her voice even. Braden seemed almost apologetic this morning. A very different attitude from last night.

Laura's attention shifted to the little boy standing beside him. Her heart clenched as her sister's blue eyes looked up at her. The child had a turned-up snub nose covered in freckles, and he was looking at her curiously.

'Hello, what's your name?' she asked softly. If her jeans had been more flexible, she would have crouched down.

'My name's Nigel. What's yours?' he said

'My name is Laura.'

'Are you our Aunty Laura?'

Her heart clenched and she nodded. 'I am. It's very nice to meet you, Nigel.' She held her hand out, aware of Braden watching them. Nigel took her hand in his and shook it politely.

'It's good to meet you too,' he said politely.

Braden smiled and put his hand on Nigel's shoulder. 'Excellent manners, Nigel. Good boy.' He glanced up at Laura and she knew he'd caught the wistful look on her face. She schooled her features into a disinterested look.

'Now, Nige, I just want to talk to Aunty Laura for a short while. You can go out and sit on the footpath and have a chat with Reg. Is that okay?'

Nigel's freckled face split into a grin, and he jumped up and down. 'Oh, way cool, Dad!'

Laura looked out at the table where the elderly gentleman called Reg had been sitting last night when he had caught her attention.

'Goodness me. He's still there?' she exclaimed. 'From last night?'

Braden shook his head. 'Don't worry, he's been home and now he's back for the day. Reg lives at the table. He goes home to sleep and that's about it. The pub feeds him and he keeps most of the locals and the grey nomies and the odd international tourist quite entertained with his history of the district.'

'I like talking to Reg, Aunty Laura.' A pang twinged in her heart at the "Aunty Laura". 'He knows all sorts of things,' Nigel said. 'And sometimes he knows swear words too, but Daddy— I mean, Dad—said to him that he wasn't allowed to use swear words when we were here, so he doesn't anymore.' He looked up at his father earnestly. 'Honest, Dad. Spit to death and cross my heart, he doesn't, he's really, really good now. Reg has learned how to behave.'

'Okay, off you go,' Braden said with a smile.

Laura smiled at him, thinking how much more pleasant Braden was without the gruffness he'd carried last night. 'It was very nice to meet you, Nigel. I shall see you again, I'm sure.'

'Yeah, you'll have to come out and meet Tweedle.' Nigel hurried out the door and soon a conversation was underway outside.

'Tweedle?' she asked Braden.

'Nigel's pup,' he said.

'Thank you for coming to see me, Braden. I wasn't sure if I would be welcome at your farm.'

He stared down at her and his face was set. Maybe the pleasantries had only been forthcoming in front of his son?

Laura kept her eyes on Braden.

He lifted his hand and ran it through his short hair. 'Righto, Laura. Let's cut to the chase. It's time to know what you're after.'

## Chapter 17
### *Braden*

'After?' Laura's eyes were wide. 'I'm not after anything. I'm just here to see my nephews and make sure that they are being well cared for.'

'And what would make you think they aren't?' Braden tried to keep his voice even, but it was hard. He didn't know this woman from a bar of soap, and it pissed him off that she was questioning the care of his boys.

Who did she think she was? And what right did she have to question him about *his* boys?

And why would she even doubt they were receiving decent care?

They were his kids, for Christ's sake. He'd walk through fire to make sure they were safe and happy. Those three little boys had had enough to deal with already in their short lives and he'd be damned if Laura Adnum was going to add to that with her unwanted interference.

He wouldn't let her.

Braden bit back his temper as he tried to figure her out, and he took a deep breath, fighting to stay calm. Losing it with her would just make her more determined to cause trouble.

What was her motivation? Was she after money? Did she want the boys? He needed to know *why* she was here. And why she'd turned up now.

'Come and sit down with me so we can talk this out.' He gestured to a table just inside the door. That way he could keep an eye on Nigel out there with Reg, and keep half an ear on their conversation. Laura hesitated and then she pulled out the chair and sat at the table.

'Laura, I'm going t be frank. I may have seemed out of sorts to you last night but what you had to say—and may I say that it was totally unwarranted—really upset me. I accept that Julia was your sister, and I'm sure that you have the well-being of my boys in your heart. However, how I bring them up and how I look after them is nobody's business but mine.'

Laura lifted her hand and then quickly put it back on her lap. 'I only want what is good for the boys. I know I wasn't a good sister to Julia, and I know that we didn't see each other much but I wanted to come out here and make sure that her boys were fine.'

Braden put his head down for a moment before he lifted his eyes and met her steady gaze. 'Laura, we've been through some pretty torrid times here over the last two to three years and I don't need you stirring it all up again. Okay, I was devastated when

Julia died and yes, I went to pieces. And I'll freely admit that I wasn't up to looking after the boys then. But thanks to the love and kindness and care of my sister, Sophie, for those little boys, and for me, I was able to get through it. Sophie took the three boys and she looked after them. She made sure that they came to see me regularly. And that was part of my healing. Now, it might seem too soon to you, but I met Callie and I love her. And so do the boys. We're engaged to be married, she's not my new wife yet, as you have heard incorrectly. She's wonderful with the boys. They respect her and she cares for them. But the bottom line is this is *our* life; Callie is the woman to help me bring up my sons, and God willing, to spend the rest of our lives together.'

Braden's hands were shaking as he finished speaking. It was the most he'd talked about Julia and the sad situation in many, many months. He felt shell-shocked after explaining it to Laura, and resentful that he had to.

It was the first time he had spoken about his love for Callie to anyone but her, and the words were said to a stranger. And he'd never spoken of that difficult time when the boys had gone to Sophie. He hated that she had made him think of that time and talk about it.

Braden sat back and focused on composing himself and keeping his voice steady. 'I want you to think about that and then I'd like you to tell me why you are really here. Is it because you want a share in the station? Julia left no will, and that has added to the difficulty of the situation.'

Laura's eyes widened and she straightened in the chair as he stared at her.

'Oh my God, no. Of course, I don't want your money I don't *need* your money. I just want to see that my sister's boys are okay.'

Braden shook his head. 'Why now? I don't get it, Laura. Why all of a sudden? Why weren't you here checking and helping us when Julia died? Why are we just seeing you now?'

He noticed her hands were shaking as she moved them to grip the edge of the table. Her mouth opened and closed a couple of times as she obviously searched for the right words.

'I can't tell you why. That's personal.'

Braden stared. 'And you don't think what I've just told you is personal to me too?' His stomach was churning so much that he felt ill.

Laura's face was white and her lips were set in a straight line, but she was immovable. 'Like I said, I need to see that Julia's boys are fine. And so far, I've seen them sent to a babysitter to stay while you and your fiancée spent the night in a hotel.'

'Now wait a—'

'No, you let me finish. So far, I've only met Nigel and while he seems to be well-mannered, where is he now? He's out there talking to an eighty-something-year-old man who swears in front of him.'

Braden held onto his temper—just. 'I beg to differ. I would rather him be out there with old Reg—who, just quietly, I trust with my son—than sitting in here with us listening to this conversation. How about we make a day for you to come out to Kilcoy Station and you can meet the three of them? You've already met Callie, and I'm sure you've seen for yourself what a lovely person she is. In fact, I believe she even invited you out to stay, without knowing what an interfering bitch you can be.'

That hit home. Her pale cheeks flushed pink.

'You can come out and you can see them in their home and you can make a judgement for yourself as to how happy *my boys* are. I don't know what your plans are even if you decide they're not happy. Do you really think I'd let my boys leave with a stranger and go somewhere that's not their home?'

Laura straightened and her eyes were cold. 'I have my reasons right now, and I'm sure if you're a good father as you say you are, you will understand.

However, I don't have time to talk with you now, or visit you today. I'm getting picked up very shortly to have a day out looking at your district. Perhaps we could organise a time for me to come out as you say? So, I'll leave that to you.' She picked up her bag and pulled out a card. 'Here is my phone number.'

Braden nodded slowly. 'I think that's the best solution. Leave anything you may believe—not that I have a clue where you have got this perception from— and there will be no hard feelings, and no expectations. You just come out and see the boys at home.'

'Very well.'

'Will you still be here next weekend?

'Perhaps.'

'Perhaps?' he asked with a frown. 'Is that because you were—are—expecting to stay at the station?'

'I was, but that won't be feasible now if I am working in town.' Her voice was clipped and formal.

Braden was taken aback. 'Working? I thought you were here on a visit.'

'Dr Higgins has offered me a three-month contract at the hospital. There is a need and I'm here, so I've agreed to consider it.'

Braden's heart sank. He had enough to worry about without an interfering sister-in-law living locally. 'A three-month contract? I thought you were on holiday. Don't you have to get back home?' He paused. 'What about . . . sorry, I've forgotten your husband's name?

Braden was taken aback when Laura's face flushed bright red and she straightened even more if it was at all possible. He'd never seen anyone with such an excellent posture.

'*Brett* and I are divorced and I don't have to be anywhere. I'm a free agent. I'm here to meet my sister's children and to make sure that they are well cared for. You don't need to know anything else about me.'

Braden could feel the anger rumbling in his chest and he ignored it.

'Very well, Laura. Depending on your schedule we'll make it next Saturday afternoon. I'll text you so you can confirm. Please leave your visit until the afternoon, it will give the boys a chance to get all their chores done.'

She raised her eyebrows.

'Yes, they have chores, as they learn about some responsibility. If you'd like to come for lunch on Saturday, you can see us working together as a family and then you can have some leisure time with the boys in the afternoon.'

'I'll text you,' she said shortly.

'If I'm out at the station or if the weather is bad, I may not get your message so at this stage, I'll expect you at 12.30 next Saturday for lunch.' He pushed himself to his feet. 'I have to go. I have a date at the rural store with my son, and then I have to pick up his brothers and my fiancée and go back to our home. I hope you have a good day, Laura, and I look forward to meeting you next Saturday. Goodbye.'

Braden turned, and without looking at her again, he went out to collect Nigel; his stomach was churning but he was quite proud of how he'd handled the situation.

# Chapter 18

*Harry*

Harry was late arriving at the pub to pick Laura up. He locked the car quickly and hurried across to the front door of the hotel.

As he walked through the door past old Reg, Harry kept his head down and volunteered a quick, 'Good morning, Reg,' without stopping.

However, he came to a sudden stop when he encountered Laura sitting at a table just inside the door. Her back was ramrod straight, her cheeks flushed, and she was staring ahead at nothing in particular.

'I'm so sorry I'm late, Laura. I hope you haven't been waiting too long. I called in at the hospital on my way through to check on the woman from the car accident yesterday but she's fine. I also called in to see Fallon and her baby. They're going well. Fallon wants to go home.'

There was no reaction from Laura.

'Laura?' Harry said quietly, as he frowned. She almost looked like she was in shock. Finally, he touched her arm and she jumped and turned to him, her eyes vacant.

'Laura, are you all right? You look upset.'

She seemed to come back to the present and shook her head.

'Oh, hello, Harry. I'm sorry, I was miles away.'

'I'm sorry I was late.'

'Don't worry. We're on your schedule, not mine, I'm in your hands and my day is yours.' She seemed to perk up a bit as she spoke and he wondered what was wrong. Something had obviously upset her.

'Bec Hunter is better today and is back on duty.'

'Bec Hunter?'

'Our director of nursing. She's looking forward to meeting you.'

'Oh. Okay. I'll go and see her through the week.'

'I'll be honest. I slept in a little bit and I rushed around trying to get here on time.'

Laura nodded but her face was still pale.

'Was yesterday too much for you, Laura?' Harry asked with concern. 'I'm sorry we threw you in at the deep end. You started off having a relaxing dinner, ended up delivering a baby, and then I offered you a job at the end. Not to mention asking you to let me know as soon as you could. It's a wonder you didn't leave town first thing this morning.' He tried to make her smile, but her mouth was set in a straight line. He could now see the anger rolling off her, and he wondered if he'd really stuffed up.

Her words reassured him and then worried him. 'It was an eventful night, but I was happy to help out. I'm just a bit upset about being told off quite smartly by my brother-in-law that I have no right to have any interest in the care and well-being of my nephews.'

Harry frowned again, wondering what had been said. Surely no one had said anything to her about Nigel. Laura had only just arrived in town.

'Is that why you came to Augathella, Laura? Did you have some concerns about the boys?'

She looked at him intently and he knew that she knew something.

'I have reason to be concerned,' she said.

Harry was placed in a difficult position. Of course, he couldn't tell her anything about Braden and Callie bringing Nigel in to see him, or about Nigel's referral to the child psychologist in Charleville.

For the life of him, Harry couldn't think of how Laura would have heard about that. Braden and Callie had indicated that for the time being, they weren't going to share Nigel's referral with anyone, not even the school. His difficult behaviour seemed to be mainly at home and in his family interaction, according to them.

Harry knew it wasn't up to him to decide what was best for the child. It certainly wasn't all right for him to discuss Nigel with Laura.

So, he sat quietly for a moment and then reached out to gently touch her hand.

'So, Miss Laura, are you ready to come on an adventure?'

Her face brightened slightly. 'An adventure?' she asked. 'I thought we were going to see a patient or rather, I thought *you* were going to see a patient.'

'That's a small part of our day and one stop I will get done very quickly. Now, if you're ready, come out to my chariot and I shall take you on a journey.'

He took her hand and Laura's face finally held a smile as he led her outside.

'Wow,' she said. 'Are we going on a safari?'

Harry nodded sagely. 'Living and working in the west means a safari vehicle is essential. A four-wheel-drive with all the bells and whistles, driving lights, canopies, bull bars, snatch straps and the works.' Harry grinned and tapped his nose. 'I know what the outback can throw at a hapless doctor from the city.'

When he'd bought the second-hand vehicle, he hadn't been sure where he would end up so maybe he had gone a tad overboard. He hadn't even had the vehicle in four-wheel drive yet.

'Madam, my chariot will take you wherever you like and it will transport you safely through flood and fire,' he said with a grin. 'So never fear, we will be home in plenty of time for dinner.'

*Love it, Harry.* For the first time since yesterday, Jenny's voice chimed into his thoughts.

He took Laura around to the passenger side and opened the door. She had trouble climbing up into the high vehicle, and he pointed out the handle above the door. 'You can pull yourself up with that,' he said. She was a very attractive woman, and the last thing he wanted to do was put his hands on her waist to help her up. It might be construed the wrong way.

Harry waited for Jenny's voice to tell him it was *most* out of character for him to notice a woman's figure. He shut the door and shook his head and walked around to the driver's side.

He thought he'd tell Laura their plans for the day after they headed off. Another reason he'd been late was that he'd run down to IGA on the way and bought supplies for lunch. The selection of gourmet food there had kept him well fed for the past month. Jules behind the counter had even packed it into a basket for him this morning. A red and white checked cloth and napkins, and some matching red plastic glasses made the basket look quite elegant.

'A hot date, Doc?' Jules had grinned at him when he'd asked her to pack up lunch for two.

'Just a friend,' he'd replied, but he knew the town would soon know he'd purchased a picnic for two. That's why he'd decided to go out of town. There was a pretty spot on a creek on the way back from Mrs Jurgens' house. It was a pleasant day to sit in the sun and have a picnic lunch. The last hurrah of autumn.

*You're waxing poetic, Harry.*

He started the car and glanced across at Laura as they pulled out onto the road. He drove up Main Street, past Meat Ant Park, but she seemed lost in a world of her own again, not taking any notice of their surroundings. Harry turned onto the highway and decided to leave her to her thoughts. Something was upsetting Laura.

There would be plenty of time for talking later. He was interested in getting to know Laura Adnum and finding out what her demons were.

\*\*\*

Laura's thoughts churned around in her head as they drove along the highway. A few kilometres out she began to take notice of their surroundings. The bush on the sides of the road was sparse and scrubby. No mountains, no green forests and no wide stone-filled rivers like she was used to, just washed-out, monotonous flat country with low trees and the occasional dry stream. She tried to focus on her surroundings and put her thoughts at bay, but it was impossible.

Braden's words had been a wake-up call. Why was she here?

She'd had no idea about any issues with the boys until that woman at the garage on the outside of town had filled her in when she'd stopped to get petrol yesterday morning.

She'd filled up the car and gone into the shop to pay, and the woman had struck up a conversation with her.

'Passing through, love?' she'd asked as Laura handed over her Mastercard.

'No. I'm here to visit family,' she said.

'Nice. In town?'

'No, but you might be able to help me. I haven't met them yet, and I have no idea where the farm is. My visit is a surprise. Are you a local?'

'Sure am. My name's Ros. Where are you headed?' She handed over the receipt with Laura's card.

'A place called Kilcoy Station.'

The woman froze. 'Braden Cartwright? You said family?'

'Yes, that's right. Is it far? Do you know him?'

'Oh yes, I know the Cartwrights well. Are you sure you want to go out there?'

Laura was quite taken aback. 'Why do you say that?'

'Because it's a bloody disgrace. The way his wife was barely cold in her grave, and he took up with that woman, and then she moved into his bed. Pardon me, but half the town reckon they were seeing each other before poor Julia was killed.' Her face was set in a disgusted sneer. 'And now I hear they've gone and got married. That Callie thinks she's pretty damn hot and she got her hooks into him quick smart. He's loaded, you know. Those poor little boys are a mess. My little fellow goes to kindy with Petie. You know, he's four years old and he still wets his pants, and don't get me started on the other two. They've turned into bullies just like their father. It's a wonder the boys haven't been taken off them, but of course, Cartwright's word is law around here. He's the kingpin of cattlemen in the district and no one would be game to put them into the authorities. You go very careful out there, won't you? You can't trust a word they say, and that sister of his is just as bad.'

Laura had put a hand to her mouth, horrified at what she'd heard. 'Is it far out there?'

'About an hour. I'll draw you a map. Maybe you're what those poor kids need.' She tipped her head to the side. 'You look like Julia. Are you related?'

Laura had nodded mutely, as her horror turned into rage. She was meant to come; Julia would have wanted her to. And if things were that bad, she'd make sure those poor little boys left with her.

Laura looked up as Harry's vehicle slowed. She turned her attention back to the road.. A stop-and-go sign ahead indicated roadworks and Harry stopped the car but left the engine running.

'You've been quiet, Laura. Are you tired from last night?'

'No, just a bit on my mind,' she said. 'Harry? How well do you know Braden and his family?'

Harry's tone was cautious, and Laura picked up immediately that he too knew what the family was really like. Braden certainly put on a good act.

Laura had even started to wonder if that woman in the garage had been exaggerating, but Harry's hesitation confirmed her worst fears.

She put up a hand. 'No, don't answer that, Harry. I know as the local doctor you're bound by oath not to share information. I totally understand.'

He nodded. 'Thank you, Laura. It was a difficult question that I'm afraid I can't answer.'

She knew then that Braden Cartwright had pulled the wool over her eyes. So much for all the happy family stuff she'd seen at the pub, Callie as sweet as anything, inviting her to stay, and Sophie being interested in her. And Braden poured his heart out to her this morning. She'd almost fallen for it.

Laura hadn't known what to expect when she'd arrived, but it certainly hadn't been this, but after less than twenty-four hours in the district in Augathella, she knew her life had already changed.

'I'm finding it hard to get used to this dry landscape. The Outback.'

'I'm barely used to it myself,' he answered.

'You said the other night you'd only been here a month?'

'Yes. It's different to what I expected in many ways.'

'Really? I thought you had been here a long time. You seem settled.'

'I never settle anywhere for very long.'

Laura's interest was piqued as she detected a note of sadness in his voice. Her worries faded into the background for a while. 'It's different to what I expected too. The country, I mean.'

'It's a big country and there are lots of different landscapes. I've lived in many of them. One thing

I've found here though, is the community is incredible. Very welcoming. They work together and look out for each other. It was all trouble-free until yesterday.'

'You mean, Fallon's emergency delivery?'

He chuckled. 'No, that was fine. I meant the gastric bug we dealt with yesterday.'

'Ah,' she said. 'I'm glad I missed *that* experience.'

The light changed to green and the stop-and-go man sitting on the chair waved them through.

'Now we've only got about fifteen kilometres to go. and I thought we might stop for a late morning coffee before we head out to see my patient. There's a nice little coffee shop there next to the teddy bear shop.'

'Teddy bear shop?'

'Yes, Tambo Teddies is very famous. I haven't stopped in town before, I usually grab a takeaway coffee at the coffee shop and go straight out to Mrs Jurgens. I'm looking forward to a leisurely day and getting to know you a bit better. Especially now that we might be working together.'

'I am too.'

'Then after coffee, we'll have about a ten-minute drive. You'll love Mrs Jurgens. She came into the hospital to meet me during my first week there and it's such a difficult journey for her to make, I decided to visit her once a fortnight on my Sundays off. She has to get the community transport down and then she had to wait for ages to be taken back home so I offered to come out and do a home visit. She was so grateful. She's a dear old thing, and it gives me more of a chance to see the district.'

'It's quite a large district to do home visits in,' she said with a smile. 'I haven't heard of a doctor doing home visits for a long time.'

'I made an exception for this dear lady and you'll see when you meet her. Laura?' He glanced over at her, and she held his gaze.

'Would you like to come to Jenny Riley's garden party with me, next weekend?'

'A garden party?' Laura queried. 'In Augathella? I didn't see many gardens there.'

'Jenny Riley lives on the edge of town and I believe her garden is beautiful, but I haven't been there. It may not be what you're used to in New Zealand or what I've been used to in some of the cities I've lived in but it's for a good cause. The CWA is raising money for the RFDS. Apparently, it's held each spring and autumn. I believe the whole town is baking and people come from as far away as Morven and Mitchell, Tambo and Charleville and even further.'

'I went through some of those towns on the way in. It is quite a distance,' Laura said.

'You drove all the way from Brisbane, I'm assuming?'

'I did. I wanted to have a car out here, so I could be independent and not fly because I wasn't—and I'm not—sure how long I'm staying but in hindsight, I realised I could have flown, and hired a car at Charleville.'

'But you got to see the country on your way.'

All was quiet again until they approached the outskirts of town and Laura turned her thoughts from the problem with Braden and the children to whether she would accept Harry's job offer in the hospital.

Laura began to make a list in her head. Think of the PMIs, she thought to herself.

*Okay, what's the first?*

The first plus is that I can get to know the boys and see for myself if what that woman said was true.

The first minus is . . . she mentally shook herself.

*Stop it! PMI?*

That had been a Brett thing; that's what her ex used for all their decision-making. And look at her now. Divorced and alone.

What Laura needed to do was follow her heart and her heart was telling her over and over that this would be a good place to stay and help herself get back to normal. Let herself heal, and help her family—Julia's boys—at the same time.

Only for a short while, but it had the best of everything. The only problem was, she had to find somewhere to stay. She would accept Harry's offer of the job at the hospital. He'd said that the prenatal clinic would run twice a week and that women came from quite a distance away for their prenatal checks.

He'd also said they had a couple of babies born every month so that wouldn't be hard work. She felt comfortable either way. Prenatal work or in the delivery room.

Apparently, most of the mothers went down to Charleville to give birth in the bigger hospital where neonatal facilities were on hand.

Harry said the women who delivered at Augathella Hospital were like Fallon.

'Fast deliveries and we don't have time to get them down there.'

Another advantage was that she got on so well with Harry, and already had a lot of respect for him.

He was a nice man; she'd enjoyed his company, and it meant she knew someone else here without relying on Braden and his family and circle of friends.

She still hadn't figured her brother-in-law out, but every time she tried to, she thought of what that woman had said and how strongly she'd emphasised her words.

Laura knew that he and Julia had had a good marriage, but he'd often been away out on the station and Julia had often been left alone with the boys.

Maybe when she went out to the property and saw them in their home environment, she would understand them a little bit more.

And then there was Callie. As much as Laura didn't want to like her from what she'd heard, her first impression was that of a kind person. Generous with her offer to stay at the station, and she'd been lovely with Fallon during the birth.

*Okay, what's against it?* she thought. Don't call it a minus; that brought Brett to mind too much.

Laura stared at the small houses as they drove into the outskirts of town. The ground was still flat but there were some pretty gardens on the right. She noticed a library in an old cottage with a beautiful rose garden, and on the other side of the road, the shire offices were surrounded by magnificent gardens.

Maybe it wasn't so unheard of to have a garden party in this landscape. Augathella must have some lovely gardens too.

'The coffee shop's just up here on the right.' Harry interrupted her musing. 'We'll have a coffee and then it's not far out to Mrs Jurgens' place. Are you happy to have a break?'

'I am. Thank you for inviting me. It's a beautiful day and I enjoyed the drive.'

'You've been quiet.'

'I've been thinking about the job.'

Harry grinned and he held up one hand with his fingers crossed. 'Good thinking?'

'I've decided to accept your offer, Harry. I'll be staying in the district for a while.'

His expression held great satisfaction. 'That's wonderful news.'

'You'll have to be patient with me. I just have to get used to living in the outback.'

# Chapter 19

*Laura*

Mrs Jurgens was a delightful 102-year-old dressed in a long paisley printed dress, with her fine white hair held up with jewelled combs. She had welcomed Harry as though he was a long-lost son and then held her hand out to Laura and squeezed it gently with her frail, cold hands.

'Welcome to my home. Now you two sit down on the veranda here and I'll go and make us all a lovely cup of tea.'

Laura glanced at Harry and he nodded slightly.

'May I come and help you in the kitchen?' she asked, not wanting a cup of tea because it had only been ten minutes since she finished a coffee and a piece of carrot cake that Harry had cut in half at the cafe.

'No, no, no, my dears. You sit here and chat and I'll bring out the tray.' Laura sat down, shaking her head as Mrs Jurgens headed off to the kitchen.

Harry had smiled. 'See, I told you she was pretty special.'

It had been a lovely visit and all Harry had done—besides drinking a cup of tea and having another piece of cake—was check her blood pressure and take a quick look at her Webster-pak.

Once he declared she was fit and healthy and they were back in the car and heading back towards Tambo.

'You drive all that way just to take her blood pressure and check her tablets?' Laura commented.

'And to give her a little bit of company. I usually stay a bit longer, but she had a quiet word to me when you went to the bathroom and told me not to waste time with an ancient old lady today, but to go out and enjoy the lovely day with my lady friend.'

Laura's face heated. 'She was sweet and so independent.'

'And she's remarkably well,' Harry said. 'The only problem is her blood pressure a little lower than I like to see. Apart from that, she's very healthy for 102.'

'Does she have family close by?'

'Apparently, there's a sad story. She started to tell me last visit but she began to get upset so I changed the subject.'

Laura looked down. She knew what that was like.

They drove a short distance and then Harry turned onto a side road, between paddocks filled with some sort of leafy crop.

'This is different,' Laura said.

'Yes, it's really pretty. There's a running creek down here and a picnic area. I have some lunch in the back of the safari wagon.'

She shot him a smile.

Harry parked in a small car park. From the car, she could see the river glinting in the late morning sunlight and hear it burbling through the small rocks.

'This is a little bit more like home,' she said. Thick green rushes edged the river and just ahead was a mown green patch with a table and a bench seat in the centre.

'You go and sit down, madame, and I shall get our lunch organised.'

Laura put her hand on her stomach. 'I don't think I need lunch, Harry. Two morning teas and it's only been half an hour since we had that yummy strudel.'

'How about we go for a walk along the river first? There's a good little walk along here that eventually gets to the junction of the creek and the river.'

'How do you know all this?' she asked. 'You've only been in the district a month.'

'I like to explore and get out and about as much as I can. I hate sitting with my own company and I don't watch television very much. To be honest, if I sit, I think, and when I think, I get angry and if I get angry, I sometimes reach for a drink.'

Laura looked at him as he looked away from her, obviously embarrassed that he had said so much.

'So, I take myself out of that situation and I've seen a lot of the district over the last four weeks. Meeting Mrs Jurgens at the hospital was good because it's taken me a little bit further north and that's how I found this quaint little town and some scenic walks. If you don't get sick of my company too quickly—and be honest if you do—I'll take you down to Charleville one day. There are lots of things to see down there too.'

They strolled along the riverbank. Harry was right; it was a pretty spot. They watched as little birds darted down to the water getting a drink before disappearing into the rushes. At one bend where the river widened, they spotted a blue kingfisher sitting on a low branch over the water.

Laura pulled out her phone and took a photo. 'I'm feeling very peaceful,' she said.

'That's good to hear. You look a lot less stressed. It's nice to see you smile. Now, this isn't a professional comment, this is a comment from a friend. If you ever need to share anything or dump anything, please feel free. I have very broad shoulders.'

Laura looked at him and nodded.

Harry did have very broad shoulders; he was a fine-looking man. Laughter wrinkles edged his brown eyes, and his lips were full and always smiling. Clean-shaven, there was a faint citrusy fragrance coming from him.

He looked casual in his jeans and shirt and she wondered whether she had overdressed. But she'd chosen the right shoes. As they walked along the river the ground was uneven, and Harry held out his hand to help her keep her balance. To Laura's surprise, a shaft of warmth ran up her arm and she frowned.

It had been a very long time since she felt anything like that when a man had touched her.

All in all, Harry Higgins was a very nice man and she was looking forward to spending more time with him while she stayed in the district.

\*\*\*

Harry spread the rug and took Laura's hand as she tried to lower herself to the grass.

Her laugh was pleasant. 'I haven't done this for I don't know how long,' she said. 'But it's very enjoyable. Thank you so much for bringing me with you today. I'm having a lovely time.'

'Wait till you see the beautiful lunch I've prepared for you.'

'I thought you slept in,' she said with a grin.

'Well, how about Jules at IGA prepared us a lovely lunch? She even put it into this picnic basket for me.'

Laura laughed again and he thought how good it was to hear her laughter.

'I think that fancy basket would have cost as much as lunch.'

'It was worth it for the company.' He placed the basket beside them. 'Would you like orange juice?'

'Yes, please. I'm quite thirsty now, and believe it or not, that walk has made me hungry.'

After a few moments, Harry put the food out on the plastic plates and poured a glass of juice for each of them. He leaned back, his arms stretched out behind him.

'Jenny and I used to do this often,' he said looking up at the sky. 'Jenny was my wife.'

Laura looked at him curiously.

'I haven't been settled since she passed away. I've been a bit of a nomad, and I find it hard to stay anywhere for very long. Going to new places and seeing new sights keeps me busy.'

'I'm sorry to hear that,' she said. 'How long has it been?'

'Three years,' he said. 'And strangely I still hear her talking to me in my head. Jenny still keeps me in line.' He knew his smile was rueful. 'Or my subconscious brings memories of what she would say into my thoughts to keep me in line.'

'Do you have children?' she asked, her expression full of sympathy and sadness.

'No, unfortunately, we were never blessed with children. Jenny had some problems and in the end, it was ovarian cancer that took her life. Way too young.'

'That's very sad,' Laura said.

'Yes, but life goes on and we have to make the most of what we have,' Harry said. 'I'll be honest. I've struggled and I took refuge in whisky for the first year, but it was Jenny's voice telling me to wake up to myself that put me back on the straight and narrow. I didn't work for all of the first twelve months after she was gone. I couldn't see the point. I found it very hard and in the end, I sold our house and tried for a new start and you know what? I feel myself healing day by day.'

Laura bit her lip and as he watched she reached for her glass and took a slow sip.

'Hearing your story makes me feel quite selfish,' she said. 'I was married but Brett divorced me.'

'How long ago?' Harry asked.

'Three years. About the time that you lost Jenny, and about the time that Braden lost Julia. Like you, I haven't coped which makes me feel very selfish.'

'Children?' Harry asked.

'No, that was the problem. Brett didn't ever want children and I wanted to be a mother more than anything. I accidentally fell pregnant about five years ago and he changed so dramatically. My once kind husband—or as I thought he was—called me all sorts of names, and he blamed me for being pregnant. He accused me of doing it deliberately, and no matter what I said, he wouldn't believe me. I'd been on the pill but when I had a stomach bug, I took antibiotics, and that's what happened. Mind you I was delighted when I fell pregnant. It was the beginning of the end of our marriage, the lack of trust and his disgust that I was having a baby he didn't want.'

'And the child,' Harry asked carefully, knowing what was coming. And why Laura was so sad.

'Oliver was stillborn,' she said. 'I still haven't got over it.' She lifted a hand and brushed her eyes. 'You probably saw me crying when Fallon had little

Ryan the other night. That brought back a lot of memories for me. I haven't worked in maternity since I went back to work. Anyway, when the house was finally sold last month, I decided to quit at the hospital and come and visit Braden and the boys. I've been very remiss and not stayed in touch with them since Julia died.'

'I'm sorry to hear that,' Harry said. 'It's a very difficult thing to lose a child and one of the hardest things a doctor must deal with.'

'I have to learn to get over it. I must. I've let this take over my life for too long, haven't I? And that's a professional question.' Laura let out a big sigh. 'Coming here has brought back the memories and made it very difficult. I've been unkind. I shouldn't let it. Harry, can I talk honestly to you without you answering if you can't or breaching any of your patient confidentiality?'

'Of course,' he said, passing her a picnic plate. 'But first, how about we eat?'

Harry watched as Laura put tiny amounts of everything onto her plate and picked up a fork.

She was a beautiful woman but she rarely smiled; when she did her face lit up.

'May I be honest with you, Laura?' Harry said after he'd served his food.

'Yes?' she said carefully.

'I tend to be direct and that was one of the things Jenny used to chip me about, but life has taught you and me both that happiness can be fleeting. I don't see any point in beating around the bush.'

Her eyes stayed on his and she placed her fork back on the plate.

'I like you very much and I'm looking forward to working with you, but I'm also looking forward to getting to know you a lot better. If you don't like the thought of that, please tell me now and I will keep our relationship on a purely professional level.'

Laura lowered her eyes and a pretty pink flush stained her cheeks. Harry noticed her hand was shaking as she put her plate beside her on the picnic rug. 'That would be very nice, Harry. It would be nice to have a friendship as well as a professional relationship and I look forward to spending more time with you.'

Harry felt like a teenager again. His heart thudded erratically as though it was going to burst out of his chest.

*Maybe it's a heart attack, Harry,* Jenny piped up.

*Time to go, Jenny,* he thought. *I can do this on my own now.*

'That's wonderful,' he said to Laura with a huge grin.

They ate quietly for a few minutes and then when they finished Laura passed her plate to him. Harry cleared it into the bag he'd brought for rubbish and then put everything back into the basket.

'Another juice?' he asked.

'Yes, please,' Laura said holding her cup out. A quiver ran up his arm as their fingers brushed.

The midday sun was warm on their backs and Harry leaned back and tipped his face up to the sun.

'What did you want to talk to me about?' he asked.

'About Braden and his family,' Laura said slowly. 'I came here to visit them and I went out to the station but there was no one home. The first time I saw them was in the pub, and you were there. I was very rude to Braden because I had been told by a woman as I came into town about the difficulties he has with his family.'

Harry nodded but didn't say anything.

'But what she told me, and what I've seen so far, are very different, even though I've only just met Callie and Braden, and then Nigel this morning. And he seemed like a sweet little boy, and Braden treated him very well. I don't know whether it was because Braden knew I would be watching, but I didn't get a sense of anything that I was told as being true. He seemed to be genuine. And even though I was quite rude to him, he stayed polite. I expected someone a lot rougher and I don't know . . . just not like he was.'

Harry sat up. 'I won't ask for any details, but I know Braden is a very good father. Callie is a delightful young woman. She's a teacher at the primary school, so as well as being the boys' stepmother-to-be when they do get married, she also teaches Rory at school.'

'She was very kind to me. Not what I expected at all. Very different to my preconception.' Laura's eyes stayed on Harry's and he found it impossible to look away. He could see her thoughts churning in her head as her brow wrinkled in a frown. 'Maybe she was putting it on so I'd think everything was all right.'

'I believe she's only been in town less than a year and that she began her job out at the station, and this isn't breaching any confidentiality, since it's common knowledge she began her job out at the station as the boys' nanny. And I've seen Braden and Callie out a couple of times and I've met Sophie, Braden's sister. I was invited out to their station for dinner. They appear to be a tight unit, a very close family who've seen their share of tragedy. I think they give a fine example of getting over sadness, moving on and creating happiness out of what's left. It's made me think.' Harry was tempted to reach over and put his arm around Laura's shoulder as she bit her lip.

*No, too early, too soon.* He didn't want to frighten her off even though she appeared to be on the verge of tears.

'I just don't know, Harry. I have to see for myself. I'm confused and I don't want to do the wrong thing. I don't want to be taken in by people who are trying to impress me. I want the best for those little boys.'

'Well, we'll see at Jenny Riley's garden party on Saturday. How about you come with me and we'll have a picnic lunch at the garden party, and we'll ask Braden and Callie, and the boys to join us? That way it might make it a little bit easier for you, rather than just being there as the outsider.'

'Thank you. I think that sounds good. I accept your kind invitation. Shall I ask Braden?'

'Leave it with me,' Harry said. He stood and began to pack up the picnic basket and was surprised when Laura held out her hand for him to pull her up from the rug.

When she was on her feet, she didn't let go of his hand, and his face warmed when Laura reached up and brushed a kiss across his cheek.

'Thank you, Harry Higgins. You're a very nice man.'

# Chapter 20

*Braden*

The boys whined and fought most of the way home to the station from Augathella.

Callie had to turn around a couple of times and chastise Nigel and Rory, but she did it very carefully when Nigel got that look on his face. He needed to learn that he couldn't call the shots.

And yes, they were being careful with him but he wasn't going to get away with bad behaviour. Even if she wasn't his mother, she still was in a position to teach him the right thing.

'Dad?' Rory leaned forward and put his hands on the back of Braden's seat.

'Yes, mate?'

'Can we stay home from school tomorrow?'

'No. Why do you ask that?'

'Because we haven't had a chance to play with the dogs this weekend.'

Callie glanced back and saw Rory's eyes wide as he tried to think of more reasons.

'Oh, and Dad, we haven't had time to do our chores. Maybe we could stay home from school on

Monday and do our chores and help you around the station.'

'Not gonna happen, mate but good try.'

'Dad!' Nigel whined.

Rory leaned back and the fighting started again but this time Petie was involved too.

'We'll just let them go,' she said quietly to Braden, her word covered by the ruckus in the back seat. 'What do you think? They've been so good all weekend.' Callie reached over and put a hand on Braden's thigh and regretted it immediately when he looked down with a smile. She had vowed to stay a bit distant until she sorted her head out, but her body responded to him automatically.

If she took her hand away it would be a bit obvious.

'I'm going to yell at those boys in a minute,' he said. 'Brace yourself.'

'Settle down,' she said. 'They're cooped up in the car, and they've been in a small house without their dogs all weekend.'

Braden nodded and reached down and squeezed Callie's hand. His fingers were warm as his hand stayed on hers and he held the steering wheel with one hand.

'I do need to settle down, don't I?' Braden said quietly. 'It's been a tough weekend, Cal.'

She lifted her hand, pushed her hair back over her ears, and didn't put it back on his thigh. 'It's been an interesting weekend. You haven't told me yet what you and Laura talked about this morning, although you did seem to be a little bit happier when you came back.'

'She confuses me,' he said. 'I think she tries to put on this hard front, but I sense she's sad underneath. Apparently, she and Brett have divorced and I've got a feeling that she may not be going back to New Zealand in the near future.'

'Does she have a house there? A job?'

'I don't know. I couldn't get any answers out of her. She looks at me as though I'm something that's crawled out from under a rock. It wasn't a good feeling, having to prove myself to her.'

Callie bit her lip, worried about what Laura's intentions were. She knew, herself, that she was no good at judging people. She'd always been a bit of a Pollyanna. She always saw the good in people and while she'd seen Laura was a bit hesitant, she'd also thought she was a nice person

'Well, she's a real mystery, isn't she?' Callie finally said. 'I wonder what she wants? Did you invite her out here?'

'I did, but she can't tell me whether she can come or not. It was all very much left up in the air. I invited her next Saturday for lunch.'

Callie rolled her eyes. 'Braden, it's the RFDS garden party next Saturday. 'We won't be home.'

'Damn, I forgot. Do I have to go too?'

'No, not if you don't want to. But it means if she visits, you'll be here by yourself. There are activities for the kids at the garden party and the boys are looking forward to it. Rory is manning a stall for the primary school.'

'I did know all that,' Braden said. 'I just forgot it was next weekend. And I did hear Ruth talking about the baking. I should have remembered that when I was talking to Laura.'

'I'm sure Jenny will have many man-type jobs.'

'You know I'll come. It's for a good cause. Anyway, Laura wouldn't commit for the weekend, because . . .' He hesitated.

Callie noticed his hands grip the steering wheel a little bit harder and she didn't think that was from the bump they'd just gone over; it was more tension.

'Because?' she asked.

'Because Harry's offered her a job at the hospital,' he said slowly.

'Wow! Although you know, that doesn't surprise me. She was really good in the labour ward. Efficient and kind, and she knew what she was doing, and I was really impressed. The only thing that was strange was when I saw her crying when it was all over. I don't think it was just the emotion of Fallon giving birth. I think she's unhappy too.'

'Well, she certainly is a mystery package, and we just have to deal with her as best we can. I have to remember she is Julia's sister and the boys' aunt. They have no grandparents, just me and Sophie, and Laura has as much right to see them as Sophie does.'

'What you have to remember, darling—' Callie stumbled over the endearment— 'what you have to remember, Braden, is that whatever Laura thinks, whatever she's heard or misconstrued, about the way the boys are being brought up, that you know they're being cared for and that they're loved. Not only by you and me, but by Sophie and Kent. Not to mention Fallon and Jon, and Ruth, and the beautiful community we live in. A community of family and friends, and she'll see that. She'll see that they are happy and well-adjusted kids. Anyone can see that and all of the town knows it. If she tried anything you'd get so much support.'

'I'm still worried.' Braden raised his eyebrows. 'And Nigel?' he said softly as there was a loud squeal from the back seat. "What will we do if she gets onto that?'

'She won't. It's all confidential,' Callie said. 'There's nothing to worry about.'

He turned around with a loud sigh. 'Nigel! Stop tormenting your brothers!'

# Chapter 21

*The RFDS Garden Party*

From Braden's memory, Jenny Riley had held a garden party to raise money for the RFDS every autumn and spring for the past ten years. The attending crowds had built up over the years. They came from all over the district, and many travelled a long way to come to the huge fundraiser.

All the shire councillors came along and entered into the spirit of fun; they were being auctioned off as slave labour. The mayor always brought the highest bids and he was always auctioned last. That meant that the crowds stayed and spent even more money on cakes, plants and crafts, with all proceeds going to the charity.

Braden nodded to Paul Bailey, the local Tourism Officer as he made his way back to the gate where he'd offered to replace Jenny's husband for half an hour. As he reached the gate, he noticed three of the cattlemen he knew from down Mitchell way, and their wives and families as they parked their red-dust-covered utes along from the entrance.

The garden party was one of the events of the year on the Morweh Shire calendar, along with the billy cart derby, the hospital ball, the rodeo, and the Easter races. The RFDS garden party was an event not to be missed. As Craig Wilson always said, 'Every person in the district could one day find themselves needing the RFDS.'

'G'day Braden!' Bob Kimberly from Happy Plains Station at Mitchell handed over the entry fee for his family.

'Haven't seen you for a long time, mate,' Braden said, handing over their tickets. 'This year, each ticket gets you a steak sanga too, so don't lose them.'

'Thanks. You're right. We haven't been up this way much lately. Since Jane had the last bub, we've been home a lot more.'

'It was a busy summer up here, too,' Braden said. 'I haven't got out much either. Always working.'

Bob's wife, Jane, smiled at Braden. 'No one misses Jenny's garden party, do they? I hope we're not too late. I stock my freezer every year with the cakes and biscuits from this event.'

'From what I saw brought in, there'll be enough to keep the whole district in cakes for a long time,' Braden chuckled.

'How are the boys?' Jane asked.

'Really good,' Braden said, a twinge of guilt tugging at him. Nigel hadn't had a good night. He'd been restless, and Braden had brought him into his bed. For the first time, he could see the sense of

Callie sleeping on the other side of the house. As much as he hated being away from her, he had to admit she was right.

After snuggling into Braden's side, Nigel had slept soundly and woken up happy. The three boys had been super excited about the garden party and Braden hoped that excitement was the only cause of Nigel's sleeplessness and nothing deeper that was preying on his little mind.

Laura had been quite amenable when he'd rung her to say that Saturday afternoon didn't suit because of the garden party, and she said she had already heard about it and assumed that would be the case. Even though her words were polite, her tone was as cold as ever, and he wondered how the hell he was ever going to crack through that facade and convince her that she had no need to worry.

Callie and the boys had gone straight to the kitchen. Callie had a huge basket with three cakes and an assortment of slices, and the boys each had a box filled with homemade biscuits apportioned into cellophane bags. Callie had started baking when she got home from school this week and baked well into the night while dinner was cooking. Braden had helped her clean up after the meal. It was the only time they'd had together all week.

'See you later, Braden.'

He gave Bob and his family a wave and turned to the next group waiting to come into the garden. He didn't mind being at the gate because it gave him a chance to see everyone as they arrived.

His face creased in a smile as Fallon and Jon walked up the road pushing a pram.

Braden sold tickets to two more groups and waited for Jon and Fallon. Jon couldn't have looked any prouder. He stopped pushing the pram and leaned forward, fussing with the blankets and tucking them in a little bit more snugly.

There was a slight wind blowing, but it was a glorious day with the promise of warmth to come. The sky was clear and the weather was going to contribute to a great day. Braden could feel the tension of the past week leaving him, and for the first time, he began to believe they could get over this rough patch. After he sorted Laura out, he was going to sit Callie down and they were going to set a date. He'd had an idea about that, and hoped she would agree.

As Jon and Fallon reached him, the thump of an approaching helicopter filled the air and Fallon looked up to where Braden was pointing.

'There it is. The boys are excited because at 11 o'clock the RFDS is going to let the kids crawl all over the chopper.'

'And Jenny has hired a photographer,' Jon said with a laugh. 'And all sales go to the RFDS.'

'She's a great marketer, isn't she?'

John and Fallon stopped beside the gate and Braden held out his hand and shook Jon's firmly. 'Congratulations, Dad, it's pretty good, isn't it?' Turning to Fallon he held out his arms and she stepped in for a big hug.

'I hear it was pretty quick,' Braden said. 'Callie's been on a high all week. Said it was one of the best days of her life.'

Fallon looked at him with a smile. 'Until she has her own.'

'Fingers crossed,' Braden said.

'The boys were looking for Aunty Ruth when we arrived. Is she coming? They love your mum.'

'She's gone to the airport to pick up Dad.'

'Okay, let me see this little Ryan James bub,' Braden said as he leaned forward.

Fallon gently pulled the blanket off the little baby's face. Braden wasn't poetic by any means but all he could think of was rosebud lips as the little boy's lips pursed in his sleep. A soft fuzz of blond hair covered his head, and Braden shook his head.

'He's a cutie.'

'We think so,' Fallon said, as she looked around. 'Where's Callie.'

'She's gone to the gazebo where Jenny's got all the food set out. Knowing Callie, she'll be making cups of tea by now.'

'I'll relieve her. I'm sure she'd like to see the boys at the helicopter. Look. here she comes now.'

Fallon waved and called out to Callie. 'We're over here.'

Callie's face split into a wide grin and she hurried over followed by the three little boys at her heels.

'Look at you,' she said as she wrapped Fallon in a huge hug. 'Skinny as ever, you don't look like you had a baby five days ago.'

'He's a week old today, Cal,' Fallon said.

Callie put a hand on her head. 'Oh my God, this week's flown. Between teaching, and a trip to Charleville—' she glanced across at Braden— 'and spending three nights baking, the time has just gone.'

'And I've been a lady of leisure, sitting in the sun nursing this beautiful young man while my lovely mum has done all the work,' Fallon said.

'Let me have a look at him,' Callie said.

'Come and we'll sit on the veranda and you can have a nurse.'

'It's a long time since I've held a baby. When Jen, my friend in Brisbane had her youngest she used to get me to hold her while she had a shower. I was always so scared of dropping the baby.

'But I bet you never did,' Fallon said.

'No, I didn't, but it's been a long time. I'll have to learn all over again.

Braden watched Callie as she leaned over and admired the newborn. She turned and looked up at him.

'Are you still on the gate for a while, Bray?' she asked.

'I'm just waiting for Bill to get back and then I'll go over and help man the barbecue when it's lunchtime.'

'After we take the boys down to the helicopter,' she said and he nodded.

'I wouldn't miss that.'

Jon looked around. 'Good crowd here today by the look of things.

'You wait, mate. It's going to get a lot bigger than this. We'll raise a packet for the RFDS this year.

Callie nudged Braden. 'Here comes Dr Harry now, and look who's with him.'

Braden turned around.

Harry had gone all out today, as the senior member of the hospital staff. He wore a pale grey suit with a white shirt and black bowtie, and of all things, he'd found a top hat somewhere.

'He is such a nice man, isn't he, Fallon? I'm so pleased he's come to Augathella.'

'He sure is, he was wonderful the other night, and so was Laura. Doesn't she look beautiful?' Fallon commented.

Braden turned slowly and thought if Laura was a nicer person, he could say how beautiful she was but he couldn't get over the darkness inside her even though she looked absolutely beautiful on the outside this morning. She was wearing some sort of floaty floral dress, and God forbid, she had stiletto heels on. Like Harry, she wore a hat but hers was a wide-brimmed straw hat with ribbons around it.

'They must've cooked it up between them,' Callie said. 'They look fabulous, don't they?'

'I don't know,' Braden said. Every time I've met up with Laura she's been pretty fancily dressed.'

He looked back at Callie as she frowned at him. 'But yeah, they look good,' he conceded.

# Chapter 22

*Laura*

Laura had been quite nervous about the garden party. The picnic lunch with Braden and his family loomed ahead, although perhaps it was a better place to meet the boys out in public rather than being on Braden's territory on the station.

When he'd called her the other night to say that he'd forgotten about the garden party on Saturday, she told him that she would be there.

'Are you coming for the whole day,' he'd asked politely.

'I'm not sure yet. I'm coming with Dr Harry,' she said, not mentioning that Harry was going to talk to Braden about lunch. That was his idea, and he said he'd organise it.

'Okay, we'll see you there.' He obviously couldn't help having a dig. 'I'll make sure the boys are clean and tidy and have their best manners with them.'

'Very well,' she said. 'I shall see you there on Saturday.'

So, despite being with Harry, the nerves kicked in. Laura had felt quite relaxed with Harry since their picnic last Sunday. He'd called her every night and they'd had dinner at the hotel on Thursday night when they had planned to get dressed up garden party style. She felt as though she'd known him for much longer than a week. He was a lovely guy.

When he opened up to her, she'd been very surprised, and she talked more about herself than she usually did. She'd skimmed over the situation with Braden because she didn't want to put Harry into a difficult position.

Lying back on the picnic rug next to that pretty creek—she'd learn to call them creeks now rather than streams—Laura had listened as he'd told her about his wife and how sad it had been when she passed away.

As they approached the gate she turned and looked at Harry and couldn't help the smile that crept over her face. She leaned into him, inhaling that gorgeous citrus aftershave.

'You really do look extra swish, you know. I thought I might be a bit overdressed for Augathella, but I only brought dressy clothes with me. The outback is different to what I expected. Not all fancy homesteads and restaurants.'

'You also, my dear, are stunning. We make a fine pair.'

She nudged him and put her hand on his arm. 'That sounds bigheaded, Dr Higgins.'

He smiled down at her and a warm shiver ran down her back. 'No, just making an observation. That's what we doctors do.'

'You're teasing me!' Laura said with a chuckle, as she held his arm.

'Maybe a little. But seriously, wait until you get out to Braden's station. I've been there a couple of times. They invited me out when I first came to town; it's a lovely homestead but it's a working station. That reminds me, have you found any accommodation yet?' Harry asked.

Laura was still living in the room at the hotel and she was quite comfortable there. She could certainly afford to pay for it and she liked the spaciousness of the room. There was a beautiful bathroom plus she had a little balcony that looked out over the river.

'You know what, I'm not even in that much of a hurry to move. The only problem is doing my washing, and once I start at the hospital on Monday, I'm going to need to be able to wash my uniform,' she said. 'I've managed to wash in the bathtub this week, and hang them on the balcony.'

'I'm sure if you want to stay there, we can arrange something with the laundry at the hospital. I would imagine they're happy to have you at the pub for as long as you want. They only get the sales reps coming through there. Most of the tourists stay in their caravans or down at the motel.'

So, Laura had decided to stay at the pub and her week had been quite relaxed.

Now her heart was in her throat as they approached the gate where Braden stood waiting for them.

# Chapter 23

*Braden*

Braden had been taken aback when Dr Higgins called him the day before and asked if he and Callie and the boys would have lunch with them at the garden party.

When Harry and Laura came through the gate and bought their tickets from him, he hadn't had time to chat because two large groups arrived at the same time.

Harry had said briefly, 'We'll catch you about noon for lunch,' before they walked away chatting with Fallon and Jon.

Laura had been quite civil to him and looked happier than she had done earlier in the week. Maybe they could get this ridiculous situation sorted out today.

Nigel had been good all week apart from his restless night last night and, after listening to the excitement in the car on the way in, Braden was putting that down to sheer excitement about the garden party today and seeing a helicopter. They'd visited the child psychologist on Wednesday, and she had been happy with his progress.

'Mate, you've seen lots of helicopters out at the station. And you've even been in Fallon's helicopter from memory.

'Yeah, but Dad this is the RFDS helicopter, it's really huge. I really want to go in it.'

'Okay, we'll see what we can do.'

Bill relieved him at the gate about fifteen minutes after Harry and Laura arrived. He wandered through the crowds, the smell of frying steak and onions wafting over from the Lions' van as he looked for Callie and the boys. The RFDS helicopter had circled once and was due back any minute.

When he got to the edge of the garden on the other side of the house, he was surprised to see three gazebos along the fence, the tables filled with sandwiches, cakes, and biscuits, but there was no sign of Callie or the boys.

He kept walking down through the rose garden and the avenue of autumn flowering trees. Maybe they should do something like that with the drive into the station. He made a mental note to mention it to Callie; she was becoming a keen gardener, and the backyard of the house was looking a lot tidier.

In the distance, he spotted her red T-shirt.

He smiled to himself; Callie had taken to wearing a red T-shirt when she was out with the boys so they could spot her easily.

He never thought of something as simple as that, and she said she'd learned that in her first year of teaching in Brisbane.

He could see her ahead and the three boys were skipping around as they walked towards where the helicopter was due to land.

Harry and Laura were ahead of him heading through the rose garden, and he was surprised to see Harry's hand on Laura's elbow as she stood quite close to him.

*Hmmm, interesting.*

It would be good to see both of them happy. Braden knew Harry had his own demons. They'd had a good man-to-man talk when Harry had first arrived, and Braden had taken him out for a drink one night when he'd first hit town.

If anyone could put a smile on Laura's face maybe Harry Higgins could. Braden would be very pleased to see that.

Hopefully, this lunch that Harry had organised with them all today would clear the air and let Laura see that they were a good family and that he was a good father, and that Callie was a good person and was going to make an excellent step-mum for the boys.

The only other thing on Braden's mind was Callie. He was worrying that she'd changed her mind about marrying him. Maybe she didn't want to start with a ready-made family. Those doubts had kept him awake several nights this week. That's how he'd heard Nigel wake up in the early hours.

Braden missed sleeping with Callie; he missed her warm body beside him at night and he missed the morning cuddles and their late-night talks before the day ended.

Since she moved into the other side of the house where Sophie used to live, a gap had developed between them and he desperately wanted to breach it.

He caught them up and put his arm around Callie's waist. 'Hello, my lovely family what are we up to?'

'Dad, Dad!' Nigel jumped up and down. 'The helicopter's coming in seven and a half minutes.'

'Seven and a half?' he said. 'Wow, are you sure?'

'Of course, I'm sure. Callie said and Callie knows everything. You know that.'

Callie looked up at him and a ripple of warmth went through Braden's chest. She slid her hand along his arm and hooked her fingers through his. Maybe he had no need to worry? Things always seemed better in the light of day.

'Hey, boys? I forgot to tell you after the helicopter's been and you've had a good look at it, we're going to have a picnic lunch with Dr Harry and Aunty Laura.'

'Aunty Laura?' Rory said. 'Who's Aunty Laura?

'I know Aunty Laura,' Nigel said. 'She's pretty.'

'I know Dr Harry,' Rory piped up.

Petie looked at both of them. 'I don't know anyone.'

Braden reached down and picked Petie up and put him on his shoulders. 'Don't worry about it, mate, you'll get to meet them all very soon.'

It seemed like there were about three hundred children waiting along the fence for the helicopter to land and Braden found a spot for his family to get a good view.

Harry and Laura appeared beside them.

'Hello. I didn't get much of a chance to talk at the gate,' Braden said. 'Laura, come over and meet Rory and Petie. You've already met this scallywag.'

'Hello, Aunty Laura,' Nigel said politely.

Callie moved closer to Braden. 'Hello, Laura. It's nice to see you here. It's a lovely day for a garden party. Hello, Harry.'

Laura nodded and the ribbons on her hat rippled in the morning breeze.

Callie smiled. 'You do you look lovely. I love your dress and your hat.'

'Thank you,' Laura said, with a smile.

*That's a good start,* Braden thought.

'Rory, Petie, come here, guys.'

They both jumped off the fence where they'd been balancing on the bottom wire, waiting for the helicopter to land. Braden picked up Petie and took Rory's hand. 'This is your Aunty Laura. She's your Mummy's sister.'

Petie looked at her and screwed up his face

'You're still alive?' he said. 'Our Mummy's gone to heaven.'

'Hush,' Braden said. 'I'll talk to you later about that. Aunty Laura comes from New Zealand.'

Rory held out his hand like the little gentleman he was and Braden's heart swelled with pride. He hadn't even had to be told to do it.

'Hello, Aunty Laura. it's nice to meet you. Are you waiting for the helicopter too?'

Laura crouched down and Braden watched the high heels sink into the red dirt. She put both her hands on Rory's. 'I'm really excited about seeing the RFDS helicopter. I hear it's a very big one.'

Nigel moved in close to her. 'It's a huge one, Aunty Laura. 'We haven't seen it yet and we are really, really excited. Do you think you'd like to come with us and have a look inside?'

His eyes were wide, and Braden grinned. Aunty Laura was a hit.

*Another step forward.*

Laura glanced up at Harry and as Braden watched, Harry nodded and smiled.

'I could spare your Aunty Laura for a while to go with you. Will you take care of her?'

'That's cool,' Nigel said. 'Rory and I will because Petie's a bit little.'

'I am not!'

'It's okay, Petie,' Braden said gently. 'We'll do something together.'

Laura glanced up at Braden and her smile was tentative. 'If that's all right with you, Braden? If the boys take me to have a look?'

'Of course, it is, Laura. We'll have a chat at lunchtime and you can tell me what it was like.

Laura took each of the boys' hands and walked down to where the queue was forming at the gate in the fence.

Harry leaned on the fence and didn't take his eyes off Laura.

Braden's eyes narrowed as he saw the expression on Dr Harry's face.

Very interesting.

Braden leaned over to Callie.

'That went well. I think she's coming around a bit.'

'We can always hope,' Callie said.
'And look at Dr Harry,' he said.
Callie followed his gaze and nodded.
'That was quick.'

# Chapter 24

*Laura*

After the helicopter inspection was over, Laura and Harry strolled along the fence and turned back up into the second avenue of roses towards the picnic area.

'That was so much fun. What lovely little boys they are.'

Harry raised his eyebrows and looked at her.

Laura looked away. 'This is so beautiful,' she said. 'At home, everything is starting to disappear and is covered with frost and ice.'

'Totally different climate out here, Laura. It's quite a nice place to live but I do believe it gets pretty cold here in the middle of winter.'

'You don't know what cold is,' she said nudging him. 'Have you ever been to New Zealand?'

'No, I haven't.'

'You'll have to come and visit me there one day.'

'I'm hoping that you'll fall in love with Augathella and stay and work here at the hospital with me,' he said.

'Well, perhaps one day I can take you over there for a holiday if I stay here for any length of time.'

Harry nodded. 'That sounds like a very good plan to me.'

They reached the end of the avenue that looked out over the picnic area. It was already filling up with families as they came back from the helicopter.

'I'll go out to the car and get the picnic rug. I've brought a couple of chairs too I think it's going to get quite crowded around the food area. Are you happy to sit over there on the lawn?'

'Well away from where the helicopter will take off, I hope,' Laura said.

'Of course. Come and we'll find a patch of lawn before it gets too crowded. One where we can see Callie and Braden and the kids when they come up.'

Harry found a patch of lawn where Laura could see the family still near the helicopter.

*Her family.* An unfamiliar surge of happiness filled her with contentment.

'A perfect spot.' Harry gestured to the food gazebos only about thirty metres behind them and then with a grin, he pointed to the blow-up jumping castle on the other side. 'Something for everyone.'

'A perfect spot,' Laura said. 'Food, children's entertainment, and if you bring me a chair everything will be *just* right.'

'Okay, Goldilocks. I'll be back very soon,' Harry said.

Laura sat down on the grass. She felt it with the palm of her hand; it was dry as there'd been no rain out here for a while. She settled down, tucked her legs beneath her and watched Braden and the boys and Callie as they walked up the avenue.

She was starting to think that she had been very wrong. She shouldn't have listened to that woman.

She couldn't understand why someone would say such awful things about the family.

As Laura watched, Nigel pretended to knock his father over. Braden picked him up and threw up in the air. The delight on the little boy's face was a joy to see. Braden's smile was wide and when he put Nigel back down on the ground, he put his arm around Callie and she looked up at him and even from where she was Laura could see the love in her eyes.

She sat there thoughtfully and watched the family interaction as they walked towards the lawn Their happiness was natural and obvious. They weren't putting it on for anyone's benefit.

Laura knew she had an apology to make.

Harry came back with three chairs. 'One for me, one for you, one for Callie. Braden can sit on the ground with the boys.'

Laura held onto her hat as the helicopter took off and stirred the air. One of the hat ribbons stuck to her lips and Harry reached over and gently brushed his finger against her cheek. Their eyes met and held, and happiness settled over her like a blanket.

She'd had no idea that she was going to meet someone like Harry in this town; she'd only known him a week and already she felt very comfortable in his company. She knew that the relationship was going to develop further, and she was pleased about that.

## 

Lunch was a fun affair.

The first thing Laura did when Callie, Braden and the boys walked up from the helicopter was to stand up and walk over to Braden.

'Braden, could we have a quiet word before we eat lunch?'

He looked at her curiously and she saw the worry flare in his eyes. She reached over and touched his arm. 'Please don't worry, I just need to talk to you.'

The boys were still excited and telling Harry all about the helicopter and how they climbed over it and how brave Aunty Laura had been.

Braden walked beside her, over to the beginning of the rose avenue and she lifted her head and held his eyes steadily, seeking the courage, to be honest.

'I owe you an apology, Braden. I'm very sorry for the way I've spoken to you and I'm very sorry for doubting what a fine father you are.'

His shoulders visibly relaxed and relief spread across his face.

'I'm so pleased, Laura. I've had many sleepless nights this week I don't know why you thought that, but it doesn't matter as long as you know that the boys are loved and being brought up as well as I can do it, and that Callie and I love them. We've got their best interests at heart.'

'That's very obvious, Braden. I'll tell you what happened because I think you need to be aware of it. I came here with an open mind. I stopped in town on the Saturday morning to get fuel and got chatting with a woman in the service station. She asked me where I was going and who I knew and when I mentioned your place, she changed. She said some quite nasty things about you and your boys, and Callie, and foolishly I believed them because I didn't see any reason for someone to lie to me.'

His brow creased in a frown. 'A woman in the service station? I've got no idea who that would be or why anyone would make up things and say things like that. You didn't happen to see her name?

Laura nodded. 'I did. I introduced myself and she told me her name was Ros. She also told me that your sister was not a very nice person either and now that I've met you all I know that she was lying. She's obviously got some problem with you.'

Braden's mouth was set in a straight line, and Laura could almost see the anger pulsing off him.

'Not so much with me, but with Sophie, my sister. I know exactly who you're talking about. Ros Evans. Sophie used to live with Jock, her brother, and there was some very bad blood on their side. When you come out to the property, I'll tell you all about it. I'm sure Sophie won't mind, but believe me, it's just vindictive rubbish.'

'I should have known better. She told me what bullies the boys were and how Petie was still in nappies because he wet his pants all the time.'

Braden chuckled and shook his head. 'Petie hasn't wet his pants or his bed since the first day he was out of nappies. He's a little champion, he's been in his little undies since he was two.' Braden reached out and touched Laura's arm. 'Julia used to brag about him at her playgroup. She was a good mother, Laura.'

Tears filled her eyes. 'I'm so sorry I didn't come over and visit, but I had my reasons. I'll tell you about it one day too.'

Braden lifted his hand and then put both hands on Laura's shoulders. 'Welcome to Augathella, Laura. It's lovely to have you here as part of our family.'

She reached up to brush the tears away. 'I'm just so sorry.'

'No need to be. It wasn't your fault.' Braden put one arm loosely around her shoulders as they walked back to the group. Callie looked up and Laura saw the relief in her eyes. She looked across at Harry and he smiled at her. She knew at that moment that everything was going to be fine in Augathella.

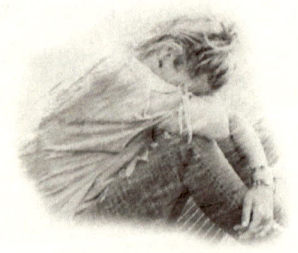

# Chapter 25

*Callie*

'So, what did you think about Laura and Harry?' Callie asked on the way home. 'I couldn't get over the way he looked at her.'

'I think there's definitely something happening there.'

'I was just so happy to see you walk back with your arm around Laura. She was a totally different person, wasn't she? Did you see her climb in and out of the helicopter with the boys? She chucked off the heels, threw off the hat and she was just like a young girl.'

'And when she was playing chaseys with them, she was a totally different person. I think she had fun too. She's working this week at the hospital for five days, but I've invited her to come out next weekend and stay. I hope that was all right.'

Callie looked at him. 'Of course it is, Braden, it's your place.'

The boys were asleep in the backseat but he spoke quietly. 'It's not my place, Callie. It's our home.'

185

She put her head down, then looked out the window and didn't answer him.

Once they were home the boys woke up enough to have a quick bath. No one was hungry, so Braden decided to put a movie on. 'We'll have some toast and Milo later.'

Callie had disappeared over to her side of the house and once the boys were settled Braden poked his head through the family room door. 'You guys stay here. I need to go and talk to Callie. Best behaviour, okay?'

'Okay, Dad,' came two sleepy replies.

Petie was already asleep in his bean bag and Rory was curled up and not far off. Nigel in his usual energetic fashion, was sitting up and tormenting Tweedle on his lap. Braden stood there for a while looking at his sons, thinking how much he had to be proud of, and how much he had to be happy about.

He left them and walked out through the breezeway and hesitated at the screen door. He and Callie had had a nice day together, but there was still a distance between them. He'd seen her hesitation in the car on the way home.

He didn't know whether to just go in or whether to be formal and knock on the door and let her come and let him in.

After a moment he decided to call out. 'Callie, are you in there?'

It was a couple of minutes before he heard her footsteps coming down the hall.

'What's wrong? Are the boys okay? Is something wrong?' she asked.

'Yes, there is,' he said seriously.

'I'll come now,' she said.

'No, it's me there's something wrong with, Callie.'

'What's wrong? Are you sick?'

'Yes, I'm heartsick. I need to talk to you.'

She looked up at him and her expression reassured him slightly.

'Come outside and sit in the swing with me.'

She nodded.

He didn't touch her as they walked through the breezeway and along the veranda until they reached the swing at the far end of the house. They could still hear the boys from where they were and if there was any problem, they were close by.

Braden leaned forward and hung his hands between his knees. He didn't say anything as he got his thoughts in order.

Eventually, Callie spoke. 'What's wrong?'

He leaned back again and put his arm around her, tipping her chin up with his other hand. 'Callie Young, I'm going to propose to you again.'

He glanced down at her engagement ring. A shaft of late afternoon sunlight glinted on the diamond. 'That gives me hope. You still wear my ring.' He held her gaze intently for long seconds and she didn't look away, but he did notice that her bottom lip was trembling.

'Callie? Will you marry me? I love you and I want you to be my wife. I want to spend the rest of my life with you.'

She took a deep breath.

'Braden Cartwright, I love you to the moon and back and yes, I will be your wife. I can't imagine life with you and the boys.'

Braden lowered his head and took her lips with his and Callie's arms crept around his neck. They stayed like that for a long time and he could feel the gentle movement of her chest rising and falling against him. Contentment settled in him.

Eventually, he lifted his head.

'Is it too soon to ask you to come back to our bed?'

'No, I was going to come back tonight, anyway. Seeing Nigel and the boys, and Laura with them made me realise that they're fine. We might need to do a little bit more work with Nigel but they've settled, and I couldn't bear to leave you all. I'll be honest. I thought about it. I thought it might be the best thing for you all.'

'And here I was worrying that it was the boys that you didn't want.'

'Don't be silly, Braden. I'm taking all of you on. I love all of you.'

There was silence again for a long time as he kissed her thoroughly. Her gentle happy sigh against his mouth had him lifting his head.

'I'm not finished. I've got one more thing to ask you.'

Her eyebrows rose but she stayed in his arms. 'Okay, hit me with it.'

'I want to get married now. I want you to be my wife straight away. I want to get married this winter. We won't wait till next summer like we were going to. We'll get married before Sophie and Kent. How long will it take you to get organised?'

'I've never wanted a big flash wedding, Bray. I don't want to be the bride in all the white stuff and with bridesmaids. I just want you to be my husband. I just want to make my pledge to you.' Her grin was cheeky. 'How about we get Aunty Laura to babysit the boys in a couple of weekends and we sneak off one Friday and get married? It will be our secret,' she said. 'Until we come home.'

'I like secrets,' Braden said, as he took her lips with his.

# Epilogue

*Six weeks later*

*Jacinta*

Jacinta Mason walked slowly out to the maxi taxi waiting outside her front gate. She could hear the laughter coming from inside the vehicle and tried to fight the dread rising in her stomach.

The last thing she wanted was to go on a girls' night out. She loved all the girls and she knew she couldn't let Sophie down on her hen's night, especially since she was going to be her bridesmaid in two weeks.

The last thing she wanted was to go to the pub to an all-male revue.

When Sophie told her what the hen's night entailed, Jacinta was horrified.

She'd shaken her head. 'Oh my God, Sophie, I'm not going to one of them. They're awful.'

'How do you know that, Jace?' Sophie said, 'Have you ever been to one?'

'No, I haven't, but I've seen them on television.'

Sophie chuckled. 'So you're a closet male revue watcher.'

'No! I'm not. I just saw one on an ad one day.'

'Well, this one, apparently, is a very professional outfit. It's like that one that garden guy from TV used to be in years and years ago. Remember him?'

'No, and I don't want to go.'

'You're my bridesmaid, Jacinta Mason and it's up to you to look after the bride at her hen's night. Kent would never forgive you if I drank too much and got sick, or fell over and had a broken leg for the wedding. It's up to you and Callie and Kimberly to make sure that I behave.'

Jacinta had rolled her eyes. 'Well, if you put it like that, I guess I'll have to come.'

Now the taxi was waiting outside her house and she had no choice. She'd offered to meet them at the hotel, but Sophie had shaken her head and looked at her sceptically. 'Nope, we're all arriving together.'

Jacinta thought long and hard about what was suitable attire for a hen's night, but in the end, she realised it didn't matter. This was Sophie's night and she put aside her doubts and fears and concentrated on having a good night.

Winter was fading and the weather had started to warm up already, so she pulled out the usual little black dress that she kept for school functions.

In honour of it being a fun night, Jacinta bought some coloured beads and fancy earrings at the pharmacy after school yesterday.

She slipped on a pair of flat black shoes because if things got too raunchy and she didn't want to stay, she would take herself off and walk home and the other girls could look after Sophie and make sure that she behaved herself. Not that she had any fear of Sophie doing anything wrong because she wasn't much of a drinker anyway.

The girls squealed as she climbed into the back of the taxi and Jacinta stared at the esky that was on the floor between them.

Sophie pulled out a plastic champagne glass, filled it to the brim and handed it over. 'Hi, Jacinta, welcome to my hen's night.'

'It's going be a big one isn't it, girls? We've got to make it a double whammy seeing Callie and Braden snuck off and got married, and *she* didn't have one.'

'Oh no,' Callie said. 'I'm the responsible married lady here. I'm the matron of honour!'

Jacinta brightened. 'So, you don't need me?' she asked hopefully.

'Even if you hate every minute of the show, it's the company that matters. We're celebrating my marriage to your brother. That's what we're here for tonight.'

'I thought we were celebrating that at the wedding,' Jacinta said.

'Don't be such a wet blanket, Jace. We're going to have a great night.'

An hour later Jacinta had settled in. A second glass of champagne had relaxed her and watching the roadies set up the show, had reassured her. It seemed to be a high-quality set and the music was not too loud.

Yet.

The lights dimmed and Sophie put her hand out. 'Sssh, girls, it's about to start. Now you all have to behave. Okay?'

Jacinta grinned at her. 'You're the one who's going to behave, Sophie Cartwright. I don't want to go back and have to tell my brother that you were up dancing with semi-naked men.'

'Oh, it's not like that,' Sophie said. 'It's a very classy show. I saw a video of it. I should've showed you to reassure you.'

The lights went out, and as they came back on a puff of smoke drifted out from either side of the stage. A screech was followed by a loud guitar riff.

All the women in the pub whooped and hands drummed on the tables.

'Bring it on,' called out Jules from IGA.

Jacinta rolled her eyes; she couldn't believe the women who were here tonight. It looked like every female over eighteen in town—and the surrounding stations—had come along. Most of the mothers from school were there, and Jacinta was sure she saw Jennifer Shaw, the school counsellor on the way in. She'd dropped her head and tried to look inconspicuous, and Jacinta shook her head. Jennifer lived down in Charleville!

Anyway, the pub was packed and there was three staff behind the bar instead of the usual one. A good money spinner for the pub and the town, she guessed, trying to relax.

They hadn't eaten dinner but Callie had ordered three bowls of hot chips from the bar to soak up the alcohol, she said.

'Good,' Jacinta said. 'Now, Soph, if I'm here to make sure you behave, I'm going to make sure you do.'

The volume of the music increased and the smoke got thicker. Suddenly the song turned into "YMCA", one of Jacinta's favourite dancing songs from back when she used to dance in her teens.

Six men—all with their clothes on, thank goodness—the cowboy, the Indian, the policeman, the bikie, the construction worker, and one she couldn't remember what he was supposed to be from her teenage memories, danced out from each side of the stage and formed a single line.

Jacinta was transfixed by the acrobatics and their dancing and had to agree with Sophie, this *was* a quality show.

Sophie met her eyes across the table and mouthed at her, 'Told you.'

Jacinta settled back into her chair and picked up her drink and watched the dancing.

The guys were in great shape and were excellent dancers.

Her gaze narrowed and her heart began to beat heavily in her chest as her gaze moved on to the second dancer in the middle.

*No.*

She closed her eyes; it was just a blast from the past. The music was firing up her memories. Opening her eyes again, she stared at the face of the middle dancer.

Dread coiled over her in a heavy black wave and she blinked to clear her vision. As she stared and without taking her eyes off the man, she picked up her drink and sculled it.

'Way to go, Jacinta!' Sophie called across the table.

Jacinta closed her eyes and put her hand on her chest as the alcohol fizzed through her veins.

*It wasn't him.*

*It couldn't be.*

There was no way that Ryder Francesco would have found his way to Augathella. And certainly not as a dancer in an all-male revue.

Her eyes widened in horror as the music stopped and the dancers approached their table.

Absolutely no way. He didn't even know she lived here

Jacinta leaned over to Sophie and spoke above the music. 'I'm going outside to get some air.' She jumped up and fled for the door.

# UNTIL THE NEXT STORY...

Callie, Fallon, Sophie, Amelia, Laura and Jacinta's stories continue in *Outback Moonlight* as we learn more about those who live in the district and those who come for a visit. Will the charms of Augathella keep them there?

*Will Sophie and Kent's wedding be the event the district is waiting for?*
*Will Laura and Harry stay in Augathella?*
*Will Jacinta get over her past hurt?*

### *Coming in October 2022*
Jacinta Mason, the kindergarten teacher at Augathella school, is horrified when she attends the hen's night at the local pub for Sophie Cartwright, her future sister-in-law. Disillusioned by a failed romance when she was at university, Jacinta is content with her life in her hometown. Meeting Ryder Francesco again leaves her reeling. His new career is a far cry from his past studies in medical research.

Jacinta is the last person Ryder Francesco expected to encounter on the outback tour with the male dance troupe. Circumstances have changed his life drastically since he had to leave Jacinta. He is wary of her reaction to him, even though he has never stopped loving this gentle, shy woman.

Jacinta is torn, the hurt from her past tells her to steer clear of Ryder, but her heart wants to dig deeper and find out why he left. He pushes her away, yet every time she pushes back, Ryder finds her harder to resist.

Can they overcome the past and give in to the love that has never died?

*Outback Moonlight* is available in:

eBook: https://books2read.com/u/meKgVg

Print: https://www.annieseaton.net/store.html

*The Augathella Girls series.*

**Book 1: Outback Roads -The Nanny**

**Book 2: Outback Sky – The Pilot**

**Book 3: Outback Escape – The Sister**

**Book 4: Outback Winds – The Jillaroo**

**Book 5: Outback Dawn – The Visitor**

**Book 6: Outback Moonlight – The Rogue**

**Book 7: Outback Dust – The Drifter**

**Book 8: Outback Hope – The Farmer**

If you would like to stay up to date with Annie's releases, subscribe to her newsletter here: http://www.annieseaton.net

# OTHER BOOKS from ANNIE

*Whitsunday Dawn*
*Undara*
*Osprey Reef*
*East of Alice (November 2022)*

## Porter Sisters Series

*Kakadu Sunset*
*Daintree*
*Diamond Sky*
*Hidden Valley*
*Larapinta*

## Pentecost Island Series

*Pippa*
*Eliza*
*Nell*
*Tamsin*
*Evie*
*Cherry*
*Odessa*
*Sienna*
*Tess*
*Isla*
*Also available in three boxed sets*
*Books 1-3*
*Books 4-6*
*Books 7-10*

ANNIE SEATON

**The Augathella Girls Series**
*Outback Roads*
*Outback Sky*
*Outback Escape*
*Outback Wind*
*Outback Dawn*
*Outback Moonlight*
*Outback Dust*
*Outback Hope*

**Sunshine Coast Series**
*Waiting for Ana*
*The Trouble with Jack*
*Healing His Heart*
*Sunshine Coast Boxed Set*

**The Richards Brothers Series**
*The Trouble with Paradise*
*Marry in Haste*
*Outback Sunrise*
*Richards Brothers Boxed Set*

**Bondi Beach Love Series**
*Beach House*
*Beach Music*
*Beach Walk*
*Beach Dreams*
*The House on the Hill*

OUTBACK DAWN

## Second Chance Bay Series
*Her Outback Playboy*
*Her Outback Protector*
*Her Outback Haven*
*Her Outback Paradise*
*The McDougalls of Second Chance Bay Boxed Set*

## Love Across Time Series
*Come Back to Me*
*Follow Me*
*Finding Home*
*The Threads that Bind*
*Love Across Time 1-4 Boxed Set*

## *Bindarra Creek*
*Worth the Wait*
*Full Circle*
*Secrets of River Cottage (Nov 22)*

## *Four Seasons Short and Sweet*
*Ten Days in Paradise*
*Follow the Sun*

## Others
*Deadly Secrets*
*Adventures in Time*
*Silver Valley Witch*
*The Emerald Necklace*
*Christmas with the Boss*
*Her Christmas Star*
*An Aussie Christmas Duo (the two Christmas novellas)*

# About the Author

Annie lives in Australia, on the beautiful north coast of New South Wales. She sits in her writing chair and looks out over the tranquil Pacific Ocean.

She writes contemporary romance and loves telling stories that always have a happily ever after. She lives with her very own hero of many years and they share their home with Toby, the naughtiest dog in the universe, and Barney, the ragdoll puss, who hides when the four grandchildren come to visit.

Stay up to date with her latest releases at her website: http://www.annieseaton.net